THE
KILLER
OF
LOVE

BRIAN CONLEY

PUBLISHED BY BUCKHEAD PRESS

3777 Peachtree Road, NE, Suite 1401, Atlanta, Georgia 30319

(404) 949.0527

buckheadpress@worldnet.att.net

Cover jacket design:

Martha James

Dawn Jones and Rhonda Swicegood - Hart Graphics

The Killer Of Love / Brian Conley—1st ed.

Library of Congress Catalog Card Number: 98-074950

ISBN 0-9664329-0-8

Printed in the United States of America
by Vaughan Printing; Nashville, Tennessee
1999

FIRST EDITION IN THE UNITED STATES OF AMERICA

To P.C.H. with love

I'm able
By means of a secret charm to draw
All creatures living beneath the sun,
That creep or swim or fly or run,
After me so as you never saw!
And I chiefly use my charm
On creatures that do people harm,
The mole and toad and newt and viper;
And people call me the Pied Piper.

-Robert Browning

Love endureth all things.

-1 Corinthians 13:7

THE KILLER OF LOVE

THE KILLER OF LOVE was a name Piper liked to use to describe himself and it had always fascinated Jimmy.

The term itself came from a song by The Clash entitled "Death Is A Star," and Jimmy's understanding of it was that it was somewhat of a riddle. The question being, "Just who, or what is The Killer Of Love?" Over the months since he had moved into the Fort, he and Piper had had many conversations on the topic.

"Is it a person?" Piper would ask. "A living, breathing human being who consciously devotes himself to love's demise? Or is it something less tangible? Like time, which has been known to wear down and wear out even the deepest, most passionate of loves until all that's left is unbearable tediousness and outright contempt?

"And what about the world?" he would add to the list. "Society - unsympathetic and uncaring like a vast, heartless machine? Or television, which bombards us with conflicting images, dehumanizing us all the while?"

For Jimmy, however, the riddle did not stop there for soon the vortex of thoughts spinning around inside his head would have him asking himself the question that tormented him most of all:

Was he just another of The Killer of Love's innumerable victims, or had he himself, through some leprous mutation, actually become this monster?

ONE

Standing at the window of his room in the attic of the HIPPIE HOUSE, Jimmy Love wiped a circle in the thick coat of dust that had gathered on the pane. He looked through the darkness at the digital clock on top of the twelve-story First American National Bank building downtown. It flickered in turn: FANB - 1:56 - 79°. Turning away, he caught a glimpse of his reflection and leaned forward to inspect himself.

"Strange," he thought.

His eyes were like peppermint stripes, red and white around the edges. But in the middle, they were gray, the color of dry ice.

"They used to be green, didn't they?"

Lifting his hands to his face he tried vainly to pull back and smooth over the dark circles which had entrenched themselves beneath what his mother had once called the windows to his soul.

"And my hair?"

He ran his fingers through it. It was darker and straighter than he remembered. It had been blonde, like Sara's, the color of honey. But now it was snuff brown, like the charred end of a candlestick, and there was very little curl in it at all.

Letting his fingers slide down the triangle of his nose he found that his nostrils were bright red and flared painfully upon being touched. He looked at his lips. They were a bruised, bluish color, and when he felt them they seemed so badly cracked that he half expected them to split apart at any moment. Folding them into his mouth, it was too dry to do them much good.

Like a splintered shadow there were two dark streaks running down both sides of his cheeks, and he felt the scraggly stubble which had been growing for half a week or more.

He chuckled to himself, like the chuckle one might hear coming from deep inside the bowels of a lunatic asylum, as he noted that, in spite of the reds, whites, grays, and browns he saw in his reflection, his face was remarkably devoid of color. So pale and anemic, in fact, that for an instant he thought he was looking not at himself, but at Piper.

TWO

Startled by the heavy screeching sound of the attic ladder being pulled down by someone on the second floor landing, he turned in anticipation of a knock on the hatch. Instead, the door flew open and Kevin's head popped through.

"I got a half-gram!" he said ecstatically.

Moving to his bed Jimmy reached underneath and pulled out the old white shoebox that held his syringes. Grabbing the two that were left, he followed Kevin to the Sunroom. As they walked in, Crazy Don was standing by Kevin's bed, playing cowboy with the .38 revolver that never left his person.

"Quit twirling that goddamned thing around, Crazy Don," said Kevin, closing the door behind them, "before you blow somebody's head off."

Don holstered the gun in the back of his jeans.

"What do you carry that thing around for anyway,

Don?" Jimmy asked warily.

Looking up, Don smiled his crooked smile, answering in his thick Tennessee drawl, "Never know when I'll need it, boy."

Making his way to the three ultra-violet lamps in the room, Kevin turned each on before switching off the overhead light.

"This is like landing on Mars," Jimmy thought aloud.

"Yeah," Kevin said, his face aglow, "but do they have this on Mars?" He held a small plastic bag half-full of white powder in front of Jimmy's face. Extending his other hand, he said, "Let's see those needles."

Jimmy handed them over.

"There are only two here," Kevin said, surprised.

Watching Crazy Don writing something obscene on the wall with a pencil, Jimmy said, "I didn't know we were going to have company."

Kevin was vexed. "That means someone's going to have to share."

"Hey, man. I can count," said Jimmy.

Like a selfish child, Kevin said, "I went to get the coke."

Ready for this, Jimmy responded, "Those are my

needles you have there and I don't think you're likely to find any more at two a.m. on a Saturday morning. Do you?"

Just as this scene was about to deteriorate into a dilemma, Crazy Don came to the rescue.

"Fuck it, man," he cried impatiently, flicking the pencil across the room in the general direction of Kevin's desk. "Let's just shoot the shit! I'll take leftovers."

"You sure, Crazy Don?" asked Jimmy.

"I got to get off, man," Don immediately replied.

Kevin was already busy preparing the coke with the tools of the trade - the spoon, the water, the belt, the cotton and the syringe - when he looked up.

"You're one crazy son of a bitch, Don. You know that?"

Noting a lull in the action, Jimmy took the opportunity to try to lighten the mood.

"Can't you see that monkey on his back?" he asked Kevin jocularly before turning to Crazy Don and mockingly chastising him as a mother would a child. "Why you're a needle pig, Crazy Don! A needle pig, that's what you are!"

Adopting a very bad German accent, he proceeded as though he were a psychiatrist analyzing a patient, "You hav a psychological need for cocaine, vich produces pheezical zeemptoms, i.e. cold svets, dry mout, und die-areea! In short, Crazy Don, you hav vat iz commonly known as zee jones."

Kevin took the first shot.

"Jones Schmones!" said Don, rubbing his anxious palms together as he watched intently. "I just like coke!"

They all laughed.

Jimmy was next.

Preparing the coke, he removed the orange cap from the fresh syringe, drew up, tied off, and injected himself. After five months of shooting cocaine the sensation was not so sensational. It was a milder rush now, more relief than anything else.

The jones had a way with time. The shots got bigger, the rush got smaller and the time in-between got shorter.

He took the needle Kevin had used and offered both to Crazy Don, holding out one syringe in his right hand and the other in his left.

"Russian Roulette?"

Squinting at him, Don reached around, produced the revolver, and stuck it in Jimmy's face.

"I'll show you Russian Roulette, boy," he said

10

gruffly, displaying his concept of humor.

"Shit!" Jimmy exclaimed, throwing up his arms and backing away. "Put that thing up, man!"

Tucking the gun away with a hoarse laugh, Don grabbed the syringe that was in Jimmy's left hand.

"You'll know if it's laced in five to ten," Jimmy quipped, referring to the fact that the needle was possibly contaminated with HIV.

"Shut up, boy!" Don looked up menacingly. "Hell! I ain't never gonna live that long no how."

"Okay," Jimmy said, shaking his head, "it's your funeral."

He really could not have cared less except that Don was about to shoot the last bit of coke.

Impatiently, Don tied the belt around his arm and injected himself. Pulling the plunger to fill the tube with blood, he shoved it in again in a futile attempt to get whatever residue might be left in the syringe.

They all called this 'jacking off'.

Tugging on the neck of his black Metallica T-shirt, Don turned flush and, just as he opened his mouth to say something, began to convulse violently before collapsing to the floor.

"Jesus!" Kevin exclaimed, and as he bent to check Don's breathing, Jimmy checked his heart.

"Is he breathing?" Jimmy asked.

"I think so," nodded Kevin. "Is his heart beating?"

"About two hundred and fifty beats per minute," Jimmy said.

Kevin stood, crossed to his desk, and grabbed the glass, which was still half full of water. He dumped it on Don's face.

Nothing!

Bending over, Kevin began slapping Don's cheeks lightly until, finally, Don started moving his lips, muttering. Leaning over, Kevin and Jimmy listened to see if they could make anything out.

"Get off me, bitch! I'll kick your ass!" was what they heard.

Slowly, Don opened his eyes and they helped him to his feet.

"What happened?" he said with total bewilderment.

"Man, Crazy Don!" exclaimed Kevin. "You did the Bass Flop! That was a good one, too. I give you a nine-point-five."

"I flopped, huh?" Crazy Don still seemed a little

groggy.

"Like a ten-pounder!" Kevin chortled, slapping him on the back.

Don looked faint again. Kevin and Jimmy reached for him.

"I'm okay," he said stubbornly, pulling away, perhaps a little embarrassed. "I said I'm okay, goddamnit!"

Kevin and Jimmy let go. Don took one step toward the door and, again, collapsed.

THREE

After reviving Don a second time, the three went downstairs to join the others. They found Joey, Harrison, and Piper in the living room, icing down the beer they had just bought at GENE'S.

"Well, well," said Piper, looking up at them from where he was hunched over the cooler. "You fellas finished fixing up with that white stuff?"

Jimmy nodded.

"Geez!" Joey said out of the corner of his mouth, twisting the cap off one of the bottles with his teeth. "I don't see how you guys can do that shit while you're tripping."

"Yeah," Harrison added, turning on the camcorder propped atop his right shoulder and crossing to Kevin. "Just how do you do it, Mr. Temple?"

Pushing the lens of the camera out of his face, Kevin made it clear that he was in no mood to be taped.

"Get that fucking thing out of here, Harrison!"

"Hey watch it!" protested Harrison. "This thing cost a lot of money."

"Then don't stick it in my goddamned nose."

Turning off the camera, Harrison retreated.

"Okay," Piper said, standing. "We're ready to roll."

Grabbing a beer from the cooler, Jimmy lit a cigarette before following everyone out the front door. They were on their way to The Grid of Self-knowledge to witness Piper's latest piece of performance art.

During the day the large concrete structure served as a subterranean parking garage for an abortion clinic, but at night the guys knew it as The Grid of Self-knowledge. Piper and Joey had shown Jimmy its true purpose one night the previous February, just after he had moved into the neighborhood.

Early one morning, two or three hours before dawn, having reached the introspective stage of their lysergic acid journeys, they brought him to The Grid to walk one of the five beams. Each beam was approximately one hundred feet long, two-and-a-half feet wide and sixty-five feet above the concrete floor.

Walking a beam in the dim light of three a.m., especially while tripping on some choice acid, was, as Piper put it, "a battle between your will and your perception."

Over the years, Piper and Joey had proven their mettle on The Grid hundreds of times. That night in February was Jimmy's turn.

"A rite of passage," Piper deemed it as Jimmy stood at the edge, gaping at the dark cavity below. "By conquering fear, Jimmy," he said with conviction, "whether founded or unfounded, all fear becomes an illusion."

As Joey bounded across the beam, waving his arms in the air above him as he ran, a lump of terror swelled in Jimmy's throat.

Having had a fear of heights since he was a young boy, the very thought of traversing this seemingly bottomless pit reduced his entire being to a quiver.

Piper took off in full sprint to join Joey on the other side, moving so fast and carelessly that Jimmy had to turn away.

Soon, however, he heard two voices wheedling him on from the other side.

"Come on, Jimmy," Piper coaxed. "You can do it! It's easy! I know you can!"

"Come on!" shouted Joey. "You've got what it takes.

Come on, be one of us!"

Reluctantly, Jimmy turned and looked back across The Grid. Seeing their silhouettes side by side, he heard more words of encouragement.

"Come on!"

"You can do it!"

"It's easy!"

Raising his right foot and placing it on the beam, he tried to swallow but found that his mouth was insubordinately dry. His heart racing, he could feel his pulse beating all the way into his toes.

"That's it!" exclaimed Piper enthusiastically. "Now you're doing it."

"Don't stop now," urged Joey. "The first step is always the hardest."

Inexplicably, Jimmy dragged his left foot forward until it, too, was on the beam.

"My God!" he groaned. "What have I done?"

Piper and Joey began to roar their approval.

"Yeah!"

"Yeah!"

"That's it!"

"Come on!"

Trying to suppress his anxiety by concentrating, he focused all of his attention on the few feet of the beam that lay just ahead. He took a step, followed by another, and still another. Stopping to look back, he estimated that he was now about fifteen feet from the safety of the parapet. Realizing that he was too far from the edge to jump back, two thoughts flashed through his mind. Either he could panic and scamper back to the wall; or else he could keep his composure and finish what he had started. Somehow he managed to choose the latter.

"Whatever you do," he told himself, taking a deep breath and continuing, "just don't look down!"

"Come on, Jimmy!"

"You're doing great!"

"Don't stop now!"

Keeping his eyes fixed firmly upon the task at hand he extended his arms to both sides, just as he had seen the high wire performers do when his father had taken him and his big brother, Jack, to the circus when they were younger. He moved forward one step at a time.

Shouts continued, but as he progressed he became increasingly unmindful of them. Finally looking up, he estimated that he was three-quarters of the way across.

"Come on!"

"You're almost home!"

"Just keep coming!"

"Don't stop!"

"Twenty feet now," he thought, and his pace automatically quickened. "Fifteen feet. Don't look down. Just keep going. Ten feet, five feet, three . . ."

Leaping to his destination, he howled with relief.

"All right!"

"Way to go!"

"You did it!"

Piper and Joey greeted him exuberantly.

"You conquered it," beamed Joey, shaking his hand and patting him on the shoulder.

"The Grid of Self-knowledge," Piper added, striking a match and lighting the crooked cigarette wedged between his teeth. "Congratulations."

FOUR

As he and the others emerged onto the street, Jimmy looked back over his shoulder at the HIPPIE HOUSE and began thinking of some of the other houses in Fort Sanders that had been given names to match their respective personalities: the Love House, the Ramp House, the Judge's House, Gothic World, and the Christian House, to name a few. Each had its own identity as well as its own story. But none of those houses, he knew, had histories as prolifically perverse as the HIPPIE HOUSE.

Noting that the two zeros had fallen off the door-jamb, leaving only the ominous black number thirteen in what otherwise would have read 1300 Laurel Avenue; he first smiled at the irony but was then seized by a gut-wrenching nausea.

Lately, these pangs of consciousness had begun to strike without warning and he was becoming less and less successful at fending them off.

Wondering what the house would look like to a stranger or innocent passerby, he could not help but fear that the place was actually a huge structure of perdition and that it represented something far more malevolent than a harmless, continuous party.

Perhaps, he thought frightfully, it was actually a mass exodus to nowhere, where the constant flow of drugs and alcohol served as the portal.

Times had changed since the HIPPIE HOUSE got its name in the late 60's when a group of true hippies lived there. Now its denizens were, in order of tenure: Joey Phillips, Crazy Don Guthrie, Kevin Temple, Harrison Cox, and Jimmy Love.

Built in the early 1900's, long before there was any such thing as a hippie, amid the shingle and Gothic cottages of the day, the house had once been one of the many distinguished manors, which made up the exclusive suburb of Knoxville known as Fort Sanders. It remained that way until the depression of the 1930's when people, no longer able to afford the upkeep on such large homes, were forced to start renting them. This was also when students of the University of Tennessee first began moving into the neighborhood, situated atop the hill just opposite the school, between Cumberland Avenue and downtown.

While many students choosing to live off-campus still reside in the neighborhood, the Fort, like many such communities that exist in the shadow of a major university, is also home to the bohemians, artists and iconoclasts of the area. And, while a number of the dwellings have been remodeled to accommodate the growing number of young residents, many other homes have been run down or neglected to the point where they are now on the verge of being condemned. The HIPPIE HOUSE, located on the corner of Thirteenth Street and Laurel Avenue, belonged to the latter group.

So why did Jimmy live there? What drew him to such a place? These were questions to which he no longer had answers.

In the past, he had rationalized that it was everything his family's home was not. He had once looked upon it as a hedonistic Utopia, a place unfettered by the hypocrisies of the so-called adult world, where everyone was free to do whatever the hell they wanted, whenever the hell they wanted.

But this reasoning had slowly dissolved over the months into the realization that he had come to the HIP-

PIE HOUSE solely out of desperation.

When he had run into Piper at the Long Branch Saloon one night the previous January and learned that Piper had recently moved out of his bedroom in the attic of the HIPPIE HOUSE to be with his girlfriend, Clarissa, he jumped at the opportunity.

At first, he marveled at the hugeness of the house. He loved its high ceilings, its hardwood floors, its intricate iron railings, and its carved stairwells. He even loved the soot that covered everything, for he felt that it gave the house a decrepit, nostalgic hue.

Lately, however, he had begun to feel differently. Unsure if the others had noticed his growing intolerance for the place as well as his increasing disdain for their entire way of life, he felt a horrible emptiness growing right through the alcohol, cocaine, and whatever else he happened to be on at the time. Loathing the cigarette ashes, the spilt beer, and the overflowing trash cans, hating the way the front porch was cracked and sagging badly, it repulsed him that everything was in dire need of repair. The HIPPIE HOUSE'S slum-like ambience, which kept the rent for the whole place down to a meager three-hundred-and-fifty dollars a month, was no longer consoling.

Nor did he receive any commiseration from Piper when he tried to explain such feelings to him.

Once, Piper even laughed and took on a mock, evangelical tone akin to the Baptist ministers on TV, and said, "What? Are you desperate for the cathartic purgation of your polluted spirit, my son? Do you feel the need for cleansing and do you long for rebirth? Well let me tell you, brother, that birth, by natural order, first requires death and death frightens us, for it is unknown to us."

Still, Jimmy felt a strange sort of kinship to Piper. They were by far the two most intelligent members of the group and although he could not fully identify with Piper's asperity towards everyone and everything, he believed he understood at least a few things about him.

Managing to gather bits and pieces over the months he knew that Piper had grown up in Atlanta. The son of a prominent orthopedic surgeon and his one time surgical nurse (now divorced), he had been somewhat of a child prodigy. After graduating high school at sixteen, he came to the University where he obtained two degrees (Philosophy and Religion) and wrote editorials for the school newspaper (*The Daily Beacon*) before being kicked off for his extreme libertarianism. Also, fighting under an alias, he had been the 160 lb. champion three consecutive years of an annual fraternity boxing tournament on campus ("Kicked their preppie-fucking-asses!" he loved to boast). And all in spite of being a tireless devotee of both drink and drug since eleven years old.

But Jimmy believed that it was Piper's diabolical demeanor that ultimately set him apart from everyone else he had ever known.

Piper's long, stringy black hair and his wardrobe, which consisted almost exclusively of black jeans, jackets and boots, matched his raven-hued eyes to a tee. Occasionally he would wear a white T-shirt, like the one which had the *Life* Magazine cover photo of Charles Manson on the front, over his wizened torso, but even that modicum of color was rare.

The qualities that made him the undisputed leader of their gang were his intelligence, wit, and primarily, his charisma. Piper often seemed larger than life, not only to Jimmy and the other guys, but also to virtually every member of the surrounding underground community. A testament to this was the graffiti covering many of the walls, signs, and dumpsters throughout the Fort which read things like, PIPER IS GOD!, PIPER LIVES, and PIPER SAYS

"FUCK YOU!" and, indeed, it was his incredible presence (for it certainly was not his singing voice) which made him such a good front man for his and Joey's band, Social Inversion.

But Jimmy felt there was also a sadness to Piper that was clearly demonstrated in his writing and in what he liked to call his 'performance art.'

Of course the others could not see this side of him for Piper would go to any length – withstand any amount of torture – to deny the existence of such a human frailty. Still, Jimmy knew that anyone who often quoted long passages from Freud, Nietzsche, and others (many of whom he had never even heard of) was not just another frivolous drunk/dope fiend.

FIVE

"I am the center of the universe!" cried Piper, gesturing expansively at the night as he began his performance teetering on the thirty-inch-wide I-beam, sixty-five feet above the concrete floor. "Everything in it revolves around me. The sun, the moon, the stars. They are part of the grand testament to my existence, commonly known as the universe!"

"Pass me a beer," Crazy Don whispered from where he was seated beside Jimmy.

"What?" Kevin whispered back from beside the cooler.

"Shhhh!" Joey turned and hushed.

But it was too late.

"Shut up!" Piper snarled, revealing his chipped and badly nicotine-stained teeth. "I call this the Manifesto of Anna Thema."

Falling silent, they watched and listened.

27

"What a tragic figure Copernicus strikes now!" Piper continued caustically. "How comical his labors in light of what Freud called the ego." Stretching both arms straight out from his sides, he began turning slowly in a circular motion. "Before Copernicus's revelation that the earth appears to revolve around the sun, the earth was considered the center of the universe."

The circle complete, he stopped and looked back at his captivated audience. "Although this theory was closer to the truth than Copernicus's theory, it too was flawed because it still did not capture the essence of the universe, which is, as I have already stated: I am the center of the universe!"

"What the hell is he talking about?" Don whispered.

Harrison shrugged in befuddlement.

"Long before Copernicus," Piper pressed on even more spiritedly, "some cultures believed that each person was the center of the universe; a divine manifestation. If this seems egotistical, that's because it is. But I must admit this was even closer to the basic truth. The only fault I find with it is that anyone who chooses to believe that he or she is the center of the universe clearly is not. Why?" Spreading his lips into a nefarious grin, he shouted gleefully, "Because I am the center of the universe! And it therefore follows that if I am the center of the universe no one else can be the center of the universe!"

Pausing, he looked down into the abyss, and, softening his tone somewhat, shrugged, "Now I'm aware this is not a popular opinion, but that's irrelevant because it is my opinion. And for those who take exception to my claim, let me point out that when Copernicus made his humble assumption that, 'There is no one center to all the celestial circles or spheres' no one wanted to believe him. The whole world was incensed by the prospect that God had not favored man.

"Oh Copernicus!" called Piper, beckoning to the stars. "How naïve is one man's search for truth when it must traverse the impetuous sea of mass delusion!

"But 'the truth,' you say. What truth? Whose truth? . . . My truth. I am the center of the universe!"

Taking a deep drag off the cigarette he held in his left hand, he continued in a patronizing tone, "You should have lived a century later, Copernicus. Then you could have learned from Milton that, 'Truth never comes into the world but like a bastard' and that 'the mind is its own place which in itself can make a Hell of Heaven or a Heaven of Hell'."

Grinning irreverently, he laughed, and, raising his voice, added with an exultant inflection, "I always say: 'Better to reign in Hell than serve in Heaven!'"

Suddenly collapsing to his knees he shouted, "I will not serve, goddamnit! I will not serve!" He raised both hands skyward. "Let the monsters, Science and Religion, battle to their mutual deaths. Yet I shall live. This shall be my motto: I am the center of the universe!

"Though bound in its physicality, I change through perception! I travel through my domain riding on the space-time continuum at one hundred and eighty-six thousand miles per second. I am the light!

"The question is not: Does God play dice with the universe? The question is not: Are His dice loaded? The question is: What are His filthy hands doing on my universe?"

Throwing his arms into the air he snapped his head down dramatically, resting his chin firmly against his chest.

Silence.

"Hey! Hey!" shouted Kevin, standing and clapping his approval. "That was great, Piper. One of your best yet."

Following suit, Crazy Don whistled through his fingers, clapped enthusiastically, and cried, "Fucking great,

Piper! That's what it was. Fucking great!"

Remarking one after another how much they enjoyed Piper's monologue, Jimmy and the others proceeded to get up and brush the loose grains of pavement from their hands and clothes. But Piper, who still had not broken character, raised his head slowly and, whisking the loose strands of oily hair from his forehead, said with vexation, "I'm not finished."

Recognizing the breach of etiquette, they all sat back down. After a long pause, Piper stood up, flicked his cigarette into the darkness below, and, continued in a grave tone:

"'Every body continues in its state of rest or of uniform motion in a straight line except in so far as it is compelled to change that state by forces impressed upon it'."

Raising his right hand, he twirled his index finger, halo-like, around the top of his head. "Newton's first law of motion orbits my brain, held to its course by the gravity of my thoughts."

Beginning to walk toward the others he shook his fist at the heavens and raised his voice obstinately, "I defy Newton and his universe of slaves! I do as I please! I'm not a goddamned machine! Defiance is my world's equal but opposite reaction to his inertia!"

Suddenly laughing, he halted, and, pounding his chest triumphantly, roared, "Fuck Newton and his gravity! In my universe impudence reigns supreme!"

Smirking, he continued in a lower, contemptuous voice, "And that brings me to Doctor Sigmund Freud who tells me I'm not in control of my actions, that I'm at the mercy of whatever goes on in my unconscious."

Laughing even louder and pounding his chest again, he cried fiercely, "Well fuck him and his instincts and fuck everybody who says that I'm not the center of the universe!

"I will not serve! Their world will not manifest itself in me! Their world will not mold me in its image until I, like some beaten and battered child, have no choice but to comply!"

Flailing about the beam with total abandon, his dark, bloodshot eyes grew wilder.

"Oh!" he howled ferociously, snapping his head back and glaring in the direction of the full copper moon. "'How perilous it is to free a people who prefer slavery!' quipped Machievelli, to which Nietzsche asked, 'Is man a blunder of God's, or God a blunder of man's?'

"Well fuck them, too, 'cause I don't give a shit one

way or the other! I will not serve, goddamnit!'"

Abruptly stopping and looking past the others, he peered into the Fort. All was quiet.

"But where does that leave me?" he said finally, after half a minute or more, his voice almost serene now and, perhaps, betraying a touch of sadness. "I am not Nietzsche, 'the murderer of God'. Ha! I'm much more comical. More cartoon caricature than philosopher. Like Popeye, a satirical rogue. I am what I am. . . . The Killer of Love!"

Once again his head was bowed but, not knowing if this was the end of his performance, no one dared speak or move even slightly.

Finally raising his head and flicking his hair back over his shoulder, he declared, "Now I'm finished."

SIX

"Wow!" Don exclaimed as they all stood up again. "You're no dummy, Piper. You know that? You're practically a fuckin' genius."

Paying no attention to this compliment, Piper looked at Jimmy. "Well, what did you think?"

Astounded by his monologue, Jimmy searched for something clever to say. Though realizing that Piper had been making a statement about their way of life, Jimmy somehow felt that Piper had been speaking directly to him about the isolation and futility he felt in his own heart. But, of course, he could not come right out and say this.

The right words finally flashing into his brain, he laughed in spite of himself, answering, "That was the height of pretension, Piper."

Piper thundered forth a peal of unrestrained laughter, "Well, at least someone understands!"

"Fucking great!" Crazy Don exclaimed, as if stuck

on a scratched groove.

Frowning, Piper walked off the beam.

"Yeah," remarked Joey, more genuinely. "I think it was your best yet, Piper. Unusual as always. You know what I mean?"

"I thought it was cool, Piper," Harrison added meekly, turning off the camcorder. "And I got it all on tape."

Unsatisfied with the others' ability to competently critique his performance, Piper shrugged and asked Joey to pass him a beer.

Joey obliged, inquiring, "How do you memorize all that stuff, Piper?"

"Didn't you hear Don?" he answered self-assuredly. "I'm a genius."

"Well, who is this Anna chick you were talking about then?"

"What?"

"Anna . . . Anna Thema," Joe clarified. "Was that her name? You said something about it being her manifesto or something. Who is she?"

"It's a play on the word 'anathema'," defined Piper. "Someone who is considered accursed or damned."

"Huh?" Joey popped off another bottle cap with

35

his teeth.

Piper grinned sardonically. "No one you know, Joe."

"Jesus Christ!" Harrison suddenly exclaimed with a chuckle. "I'm tripping my ass off."

"Yeah, college boy," laughed Don, raising his bottle as if making a toast. "You and me both."

Nodding his agreement with them, Jimmy felt his own reality changing from one moment to the next.

"This is kick ass blotter," said Kevin, to let everyone know he felt the same.

"Okay," Piper said, after taking a gulp of beer and lighting another cigarette. "We're going to play a game and it's called, I'VE SEEN."

"What?" Jimmy asked.

"I'VE SEEN," answered Piper. "Now listen up. This is how it works. We sit in a circle and go in turns. When it's your turn you have to tell us something you've seen and it has to be something that's either gross, weird, or sexually explicit. Like, if it's my turn, I might say . . . uh . . . I've seen a guy who took it up the ass so often he lost control of his bowel muscles and shit all over himself all the time, which would pretty much cover all three."

"Eeeww God!" cried Harrison. "That's disgusting.

Did you really see that?"

"Yeah. I did as a matter of fact," Piper said keenly. "Now, does everyone understand?"

"I think so," Jimmy said.

"Okay then," said Piper. "But you only have ten seconds to say what you've seen when it's your turn, and there's no lying and there's no repeating yourself or saying the same thing someone else has said. If you do or if your time runs out, then you're out and you know what that means."

"What?" Harrison asked naïvely.

"That means that you have to traverse The Grid of Self-knowledge," Piper answered, curling his lips. "And that's always fun when you're tripping your ass off. Isn't it, Joey?"

"More fun than should be humanly possible," answered Joey facetiously.

"Hey, wait a minute," Harrison said in protest, backing away. "I'm not walking across that thing. I wouldn't even do it sober, much less when I might freak out half-way across. Forget it."

"Well," said Piper in a tone of subtle coercion, "then you had better be quick because if you aren't and then you don't cross the beam, we're going to tell all those little coeds of yours what a coward you are."

"Yeah, right," Harrison laughed.

"Oh, don't pay him no mind," Crazy Don chimed in. "He's one of those college pussies, Piper. Fuck him if he don't wanna . . ."

"No," interrupted Piper with a wave of his hand, looking straight into Harrison's eyes. "I don't think he is, Don. I think he's got what it takes. What do you think, Joe?"

Joey frowned. "I don't know. What do you think, Jimmy?"

"Uh," Jimmy said, looking at Harrison and assessing the situation. "I think he can do it."

"Yeah!" Piper interjected, reaching out and grabbing Harrison by the shoulder. "You bet your ass he can do it. See Harrison? There's your vote of confidence."

Utterly baffled, Harrison shrank in reluctant appeasement and they all sat down at the edge of The Grid once more. Clockwise it was Piper, Crazy Don, Kevin, Joey, Harrison, and Jimmy.

SEVEN

"All right," Piper said imaptiently. "Your turn, Don."

Everyone focused his attention on Crazy Don, the little guy with the freckles and strawberry blonde hair which curled halfway down his back. The cowboy among them as well as the resident psychotic, Don practically grew up in the juvenile ward of the Knox County Correctional System. He had been in and out of jail ever since turning eighteen.

Furthermore, he professed to have gotten away with much more than the petty assaults and thefts for which he had done time, even claiming to have killed two men. One with an eight inch hunting knife and the other with the .38 revolver he was so recently waving in Jimmy's face.

A few years back one of Don's biker buddies dared him to shoot an old bum who was passed out in an alley, and not being one to back down from a dare he stuck the gun to the old man's temple and pulled the trigger.

"What the hell was I supposed to do?" he often asked with frightening sincerity. "The motherfucker dared me."

"Better hurry, Don," Piper warned.

"Uh . . . uh . . . shit," Don stuttered before blurting out just in the nick of time, "I've seen a man bleed to death."

There was a moment of silence while they all tried to picture this.

"I don't know," said Joey at last. "We may have to have a judge's ruling on that. What do you think, Piper?"

"Hey wait a minute!" cried Crazy Don objectionably. "That's gross. You don't think that's gross? Seein' all that blood? Watchin' 'em turn blue and hearin' that weird gurglin' sound when their lungs fill up with the shit? It's pretty fuckin' foul; I'm here to tell ya. You tell 'em, Piper. You were there. Hell! You were here, man. It happened right here."

They all knew that Don was referring to the gruesome history behind The Grid of Self-knowledge.

Four years earlier this structure had actually been the foundation for GENE'S CORNER GROCERY and, on top of GENE'S, PARTY WORLD. Legend had it that PARTY WORLD was a junkie's dream, or nightmare as the

40

case may have been. Needles and spoons, dried blood, Shannon the Hippie, Bonehead, Doc Shock, Casper, Speedy, Crazy Don and Piper – PARTY WORLD.

The details had become jumbled over the years, but Fort Sanders lore had established a few accepted facts. Basically the incident seemed to have involved Don, the Hippie, mushrooms and/or LSD, a guitar, and the hunting knife. Put all of these things into a pressure cooker and the result would probably resemble what actually took place.

One day Don became irritated over the question of who possessed and/or who had permission to play a certain guitar. Unfortunately for Shannon the Hippie, he happened to be playing it at the time. Perhaps words were exchanged? Perhaps not? Whatever happened, when it was over the Hippie had been stabbed with the knife over fifty times in the chest, neck and shoulders.

What transpired afterwards was still a topic of great controversy. The Hippie was never heard from again, and owing to the fact that he was a junkie, who had landed at PARTY WORLD straight off the road one day, no one missed him. Of course the guys had all heard the obligatory rumors of midnight burials in the Smoky Mountains and of cement shoes at the bottom of the Tennessee River, but Jimmy suspected that only Piper and Crazy Don knew for sure what happened to the Hippie that night.

The first time Jimmy ever met Piper was shortly after that 'incident,' as it was euphemistically called. He and Carl White (sophomores in high school at the time) were headed downtown to do some skateboarding at the World's Fair site when Carl said he wanted to stop by an apartment in the Fort, which turned out to be PARTY WORLD.

Never seeing any place quite like it, Jimmy was both fascinated and scared. He and Carl and their friends at school exhibited an anti-social, counter-everything attitude, but at night went home to their families in posh West Knoxville. Not the guys at PARTY WORLD. These guys were the real thing. They were living it!

They were only there for about five minutes, but that was more than enough time for the place to make an indelible impression upon Jimmy. A guy who looked like Messy Marvin from the Hershey Chocolate commercials was crawling around searching desperately for something and rambling on about a Crazy Don who, apparently, had stabbed someone repeatedly two nights earlier in that very apartment.

Messy Marvin had a wild, paranoid look in his eyes,

and Carl kept glancing back at Jimmy with a 'get a load of this dude' smile on his face. Enter Piper.

"Piper!" Messy Marvin exclaimed. "Thank God! Where the hell have you been, man?"

Not answering, Piper looked at Carl and Jimmy.

"You know Carl," Messy Marvin said from the floor, "and . . . uh . . . what did you say your name was, kid?"

"Uh . . . it's Jimmy," he replied cautiously, giving Piper a furtive glance.

Quickly walking right past him Piper bellowed, "What the fuck are you doing, Speedy? Get up off the fucking floor!"

"Blood, Piper," explained Speedy timidly, pushing himself off his hands and knees. "What if the cops come and find blood microbes or something? They've got shit that can detect those things, you know? Even if you can't see 'em, Piper."

Pointing back at Carl and Jimmy, Piper bit his lip, inquiring, "What do they know?"

Obviously rattled, Speedy remained silent.

"What did you tell them?" Piper demanded angrily, grabbing him by the collar and shoving him back against the wall.

43

Jimmy glanced sideways at Carl to see if he thought they should make a run for the stairs, but Carl was frozen.

"Nothing!" cried Speedy. "I didn't tell them anything, Piper. I swear to God! I didn't tell them shit. Right, guys?"

"Yeah," Carl said innocently. "He didn't tell us anything, Piper."

Keeping his mouth shut, Jimmy tried his best to look naïve as Piper looked him over assiduously. But Piper let go of Speedy and walked straight towards him.

Although he was not physically imposing there was something very chaotic and dangerous about Piper. His hair was bright yellow and pink at that time and his features were pallid and ultra-emaciated. But it was his eyes that struck a chord of terror in Jimmy. They were wild, piercing black slits into which the very light of the world seemed to lose its form.

He got right in Jimmy's face, and said, "You better be on your way, junior!"

Jimmy looked over at Carl, already making his way towards the door.

"Yeah, Jimmy," he said hastily. "We have to be going now. Come on."

44

"Right," Jimmy agreed instantaneously, joining him.

Carl opened the door and they were out in a flash.

On their way down the stairs Jimmy could hear Piper chastising Speedy unmercifully, but he was much too scared and excited to make out exactly what was being said.

"Can you believe that shit?" Carl said, wide-eyed, as they emerged onto the street.

"What the hell is that place?" Jimmy gasped, laughing nervously.

"That's PARTY WORLD," answered Carl.

Four years later Jimmy was sitting next to the same Piper, relating to him. Piper had given up his psychedelic hair, but nothing else seemed to have changed. He was still the same doggedly sinister Piper: a junkie, a nihilist, a misanthrope. But to have labeled him, even so extremely, was to do him injustice; just as to say that he did not believe in anything was misleading.

Practicing a sort of twisted Zen philosophy, Piper believed that he and the universe were one. The catch was that he considered the universe to be an ugly, filthy, vile place and everything in it, including himself, ugly, filthy, and vile.

Knowing this, Jimmy thought it little wonder that

he was obsessed with rats.

Piper had lived in the HIPPIE HOUSE since PARTY WORLD burned down, taking GENE'S along with it. This mishap had occurred a couple of months after the incident between Don and the Hippie.

The cause of the fire was never determined, but it is not hard to imagine how such a thing might have started in an apartment full of smacked-out junkies.

Of course Crazy Don maintained that Gene had the place torched to collect the insurance money, and as proof he pointed to the fact that Gene's coverage had been enough to not only help him reestablish his grocery, but also allowed him to open an adjoining restaurant.

In any case, Gene was covered and the guys at PARTY WORLD were not. So Piper and Don moved into the HIPPIE HOUSE with Joey. Like Jimmy, Kevin and Harrison came later.

When Piper left, he moved two blocks up Laurel Avenue. His girlfriend, Clarissa, had found a vacant basement in a dilapidated old house, talking the owner into letting them rent it for one-hundred-and-fifty dollars a month.

The place was damp, fetid, and so severely run down that everyone referred to it as 'The Dungeon'. Jimmy felt that it was the perfect setting for Piper to practice what he preached.

The first time he was ever there, he and Piper were sitting on the third or fourth-hand couch that had come with the place. Taking a pinch of marijuana out of a bag, Piper stuck out his hand and called, "Oscar! Come here, Oscar!"

Assuming Piper had a dog or cat he liked to get stoned Jimmy was amazed when a rat the size of a squirrel came scurrying out of the bedroom, jumping right onto the coffee table.

"He loves this shit," Piper declared with a mischievous grin, feeding the grass to the rodent.

Shocked speechless, Jimmy was repulsed by the creature whose tail switched back and forth as it snorted and gnawed at the pot. But the supple smile, which formed almost imperceptibly across his lips, betrayed the fact that he was somewhat amused.

Suddenly, Clarissa (who looked more or less like the female version of Piper - Helter Skelter) came barging out of the bedroom.

"I can't believe you," she chastised Piper, bending to collect the rat. "Come here, Oscar," she continued in baby talk, reaching down and allowing the creature to run up her arm onto her shoulder. "Don't you feed him that. It's cruel. Oscar, yeah. Don't you eat that, Oscar. It's bad for you. Yes it is. Come on you little fuzzy thing, you."

Piper laughed as Clarissa moved off with the rodent, cuddling it and baby-talking to it all the while.

"Aw, come on," he pleaded. "Can't the little guy have any fun?"

Soon afterwards Jimmy discovered that Piper and Clarissa were actually breeding these creatures, which he thought was probably not very difficult since the place was most likely infested to begin with.

EIGHT

"Okay, Don," Piper said. "We'll count it this time but you can do better than that. Your turn, Kevin."

Kevin was ready. "I've seen a woman bleed during menstruation."

Joey's turn.

"I've seen stitches between a woman's legs."

"Uh . . . well . . . uh," Harrison began to stutter before blurting out, "I've seen a woman have an orgasm."

Jimmy's turn.

"I've seen a woman have sex with another woman."

"All right!" Crazy Don chuckled, saluting Jimmy with his beer. "Now you're talkin'."

"I've seen a man have sex with another man," Piper said in turn, bursting Don's bubble.

"I've seen a man have sex with a woman," Don grumbled.

"I've seen dogs have sex," said Kevin from beneath

the brim of his baseball cap.

Joey's turn again.

He sighed, "I've seen a girl have sex with a dog."

This would probably have come as a shock if they all had not heard the story a hundred times of how the HIPPIE HOUSE was the only house in Fort Sanders to actually have a clause in its lease agreement expressly prohibiting 'perverted sex acts of any kind.'

From what Piper and Joey had told Jimmy, this codicil had been written in after a party where a girl actually performed the sex act with a German Shepherd. According to Piper, it happened in the living room. The girl fondled the dog until he became aroused and then, lifting her skirt, she got down on all fours. The dog, Joey explained, just seemed to know what to do. And the people watching? Well, most were either 'whooping it up' and 'egging it on' or else were 'too shocked' to do anything. Finally, Clarissa, coming downstairs to find out what all the commotion was about, saw what was going on and broke it up. The story got around, however, and that was when the clause came into being.

"I've seen a woman with a broken blister on her vagina," Harrison said boldly.

"That's it," Kevin clapped. "Now you're getting the

50

hang of it."

"I've seen a woman masturbate in front of an audience for a beer," Jimmy said, after searching the perverted recesses of his memory.

"Good one," said Joey, nodding his head as everyone seemed to agree.

"I've seen a man masturbate while looking at a deer," said Piper, expounding upon Jimmy's theme.

"I've seen a man kill a cat," Don said, changing direction.

Kevin's turn.

A carpetbagger from Chicago, Kevin was a crude individual by anyone's standards. An 'obnoxious loud mouth,' as Don liked to call him, he was the only clean-cut guy among the group due to the fact that he worked, ironically, for the Fraternal Order of Police.

At twenty-five Kevin was the supervisor of the F.O.P.'s phone solicitation office downtown, and it was easy for the others to see how his gift for gab helped him succeed at his job, which he seemed to take seriously. But Jimmy's theory was that, since cocaine was the only other thing Kevin took seriously, the job was mainly just a means to an end.

Kevin resided on the second floor in the room called the 'Sunroom.' Jimmy had lived in the house nearly three weeks before discovering its secret.

One night, as he and Harrison sat in the attic sharing a bottle of Southern Comfort while listening to The Stranglers, Kevin popped up saying he had something to show them. They followed him to the Sunroom, so-called because there was a large bay window in its center which faced due east, so that the sun would shine directly through in the mornings.

Kevin had hung four large, dingy bath towels over the sash and had decorated the room with three ultra-violet lamps, spacing them strategically from one end to the other. As they entered, he turned on each lamp before flicking off the overhead light. The atmosphere grew almost surreal as Harrison and Jimmy watched him go to his desk, open the top drawer, and produce a spoon, a belt, and some cotton. Laying the paraphernalia on top of the desk, he motioned for the others to sit down on the bed, saying that he would be back momentarily. He returned about thirty seconds later with a glass of water, kicking the door shut behind him.

At that time Harrison was also rather new to the house, having moved in only a month before Jimmy, and neither of them knew precisely what was going on. They watched Kevin go back to his desk, set the glass down, and open another drawer. He pulled out a quarter-gram of coke and a little tube with a bright orange cap on its end. After pouring the drug into the spoon he took off the cap, and Jimmy saw that the tube was a syringe with a three-quarter inch needle. Realizing now what had been going on all this time, he looked at Harrison, but Harrison was fixated on Kevin, drawing water into the syringe before squirting it into the spoon.

After stirring the white powder into the liquid, Kevin held the spoon towards them. "That's good coke. If the water turns clear without any heat under it, it's good coke."

Jimmy and Harrison nodded.

"Okay," Kevin smiled his salesman's smile. "Who wants it?"

Jimmy shrank away. Although he had snorted cocaine many times in the past he had never shot up before.

"Uh," he said. "I don't know, man. I've got to think about that, you know?"

"Yeah," Harrison agreed.

"Oh, come on," Kevin cajoled. "You wouldn't decline my hospitality, would you? But I understand. I was scared, too, at first. But there really is nothing like it, I'm telling you. Here, I'll go first."

They watched intently as he drew the coke into the syringe, tied the belt around his arm, stuck the needle in, and pulled out the plunger - filling the tube with blood to ensure that he had hit a vein. Looking at them, he smiled and pushed in the entire contents.

Turning flush red, Kevin's smile broadened. "Aw, man! Whew! Now that's the real thing, fellas. The pause that refreshes."

This was enough for Jimmy.

"Okay," he said, standing at attention like some patriot ready to sacrifice life or limb for the cause. "I want one."

Feeling his heart race as Kevin tied the belt around his arm he began to have second thoughts. Part of him said no, but another part (the insatiable one that had been winning these battles the past three years), said, "Hell yes!"

Seeing his own blood fill the tube as Kevin stuck him with the needle, he began to feel squeamish.

"Ready?" Kevin asked.

Looking up at him Jimmy's knees started to shake so badly that he felt as though they might buckle.

"Yeah," he muttered at last, gritting his teeth. "Go ahead."

He closed his eyes as the cool sensation of the liquid was dispensed into his arm. Kevin untied the belt. A fragrance, like alcohol fumes, began to permeate him and he was overwhelmed by an intense feeling of excitement, like a huge rush of adrenaline, only much more soothing. Orgasmic!

His eyes opened and he staggered to the bed, bracing himself against the headboard.

"Wow!" was all he could say.

"Well?" Kevin said, still smiling, bending to look him in the eye. "How is it?"

A smile of his own spread across Jimmy's lips.

"It's kick ass, man."

Harrison did a shot. Kevin took another and then asked Jimmy if he would like one more.

"Thanks," he said, "but no."

Convincing himself that he was just experimenting and that he was not completely out of control, he actually felt proud of himself for turning down that second shot. Still, it would not be long before 'Mr. Jones,' (the name the guys gave to their persistent cravings for instant gratification) would have him firmly in his grasp.

Late one afternoon, about two weeks later, Joey, Harrison, Kevin, and Jimmy decided to go camping in the mountains. Their plan was to buy three or four cases of beer, make it to Sevier County before nightfall, set up camp, drink, and in the morning, scour the area in search of magic mushrooms. Harrison said he knew where they grew in droves and they were all excited by this prospect.

Stopping at a little market on Chapman Highway, they bought the beer before proceeding through Sevierville to Pigeon Forge where they turned off onto Wears Valley Road. Driving a few more miles, they parked and hiked about a half-mile into the woods before making camp. After building a fire, Joey entertained the others by playing his acoustic guitar while they all drank, sang, told stories, and participated in all the customary camping rites.

Jimmy welcomed this respite from the HIPPIE HOUSE, the peacefulness of the mountains standing in such contrast to his life in the city.

At about ten-thirty, however, Kevin pulled out his little bag of white powder. Jimmy watched as he took his car key, dipped it in, brought it out carefully to his nose, and inhaled.

Kevin offered Joey a 'key bump,' then Harrison, and, finally, Jimmy. All accepted.

After that round, they continued to drink and sing. But, when Kevin reproduced the bag, everything came to a halt. This time everyone took two key bumps. Joey started playing once more but, by now, Jimmy's mind was completely on the cocaine. He watched and waited anxiously for Kevin to again pull out his little pouch of goodies.

After about twenty minutes, it appeared. Pleased to observe that there was still a considerable amount of coke (about three-quarters of a gram according to his estimation), Jimmy knew that by the end of the evening they would be licking and scraping that bag for any residue they could find.

Kevin took a couple of bumps. Joey, Harrison, and Jimmy followed suit. It was getting increasingly difficult for Jimmy to wait his turn, but the others seemed just as anxious. When his turn finally came and went, Kevin took two more bumps before passing the bag around once more. Again and again the bag went around. It had started and now Jimmy knew beyond any doubt that it would not stop until every last molecule of that cocaine was gone. There were no more songs or stories, and the drinking was relegated to performing the service of tiding the guys over between bumps.

It was one-thirty when Kevin licked his finger, rubbed the bag and 'freezed' the last particles of cocaine between his tongue and upper lip. At two o'clock they were all in their sleeping bags, grinding their teeth, about as far away from sleep as is humanly possible. By two-thirty Jimmy was craving more coke so badly that he felt like jumping up and running out of the woods to find some. A few anxious moments later he felt someone tugging at him.

"You're not asleep, are you?" Kevin asked.

"Is that a joke?" Jimmy replied, rolling over.

"Man!" Kevin said, rubbing his face nervously with his sweaty palm. "I've got to get out of here. I want to go back to the house. I'm wired to the gills."

"It must be close to three o'clock," Jimmy pointed out.

"I don't give a shit what time it is!" Kevin exclaimed, shaking from head to toe. "I want to go back now."

"Well," said Jimmy, running a cautious hand through his hair. "Tell Joey."

Shaking his head Kevin looked over at Joey, lying only a few feet away.

58

"Okay," he said at last. "But I need you to back me up because it'll piss him off."

"Yeah," Jimmy said. "But you drove, Kevin. He's not going to let you leave him out here."

"Just back me up, okay? I've got some more coke back at the house and when we get back we'll do it right. Just you and me if you back me up."

'Do it right'. Jimmy knew what that meant, and, though he feigned reluctance, agreed.

Kevin was right. Joey was pissed when they told him they were leaving. Still, he and Harrison really had no choice. Unless they wanted to walk back they had to go with Kevin and Jimmy, so they piled into the back seat as Kevin and Jimmy got in the front. Harrison went right to sleep, but Joey, still incensed, berated them the whole way back.

"You fucking pussies!" he said. "Can't spend the night away from your precious coke, huh? How sweet! You girls are really something, you know that?"

Kevin and Jimmy did not care. They did not even hear Joey, really, having only one thing on their minds.

When they finally arrived back at the HIPPIE HOUSE, Joey (still muttering expletives) went into his room

59

on the first floor, slamming the door behind him. Harrison (still half-asleep) made his way up to his room on the second floor while Kevin and Jimmy (wide-eyed) continued into the Sunroom.

Kevin prepared the coke and gave Jimmy the first shot.

"Thanks for standing by me," he said.

"No problem," said Jimmy, pushing in the plunger.

After that first all-nighter of coke, things really began to decline for Jimmy. Mr. Jones had gotten a firm hold on him and cocaine began to rule his life. Doing coke or thinking of doing it preoccupied his every waking moment.

Money became equated with cocaine. Twenty dollars was just shy of a quarter-gram. Thirty: a six-pack and a quarter. Anything over a hundred had the potential to become a private party. After having once loved company, he stopped enjoying having others around because what used to be a large amount of the drug began to seem insufficient. When he used to just snort, a gram would last an entire evening but after he started shooting up, a gram would last an hour or an hour and a half at the outside. And he would be out a hundred dollars.

His binges started lasting two nights instead of one,

and each time the first shot would be great, but those that followed would fall short of his expectations. Later, he would make conscious efforts to let time lapse between shots, but once he got high, not five minutes would pass before he would start watching the clock. Getting the rush, he would watch and wait but while the high was short-lived, the effects on his respiratory and nervous systems remained. Compounded by anxiety, this made him a walking time bomb; still wired, but without relief.

Thinking another shot would fix things, he would always find that, by the time he did another, he was so bent out of shape from being forced to wait, that his body barely noticed the coke. Then he would say to himself, "Well, that was a wasted shot and I've spent all my money for nothing" - the whole time his heart beating one hundred and seventy times per minute.

Next, he would begin pacing the room looking for something (he was never sure what), thinking he might have misplaced some money (which he knew he had just spent). Then he would vacillate between thinking that he saw some coke that had been spilled on the floor (which he knew was not there) and feeling that his teeth were about to break from clinching them (because he could not feel them). He would then get a nervous feeling of disappointment which would turn into an overwhelming anxiety, growing gradually worse until finally, and mercifully, he would pass out from exhaustion.

NINE

"I've seen a man sling a cat by the neck until it broke," Kevin said.

"Hey," protested Joey, waving his hand. "That's a repeat. Don just said he'd seen a man kill a cat."

"No way," Kevin said in his own defense. "Don said he saw a man kill a cat, but he didn't say how."

"That's a repeat."

"No way, Joe. No fucking way."

"Okay," Joey said. "I've seen a cat die and then shit on himself. How's that?"

"Fine," said Kevin.

Harrison's turn.

"I've seen a man beat a woman."

Spewing out a mouthful of beer, Don interjected, "What the hell is that?"

"What?" said Harrison, throwing up his arms.

"Now if you tell me that's gross, weird or sexually

63

. . . uh . . . uh . . . goddamn! What's that other word, Piper?"

"Explicit."

"Yeah, yeah. That's it. Gross, weird, or esplisid. If you tell me that's gross, weird, or esplisid, then I'll kick your ass."

"Well," said Harrison, taking genuine offense. "It's just as good as some of the lame shit you've seen, Don."

"Touché," Piper laughed. "Your turn, Jimmy."

Don fumed.

"I've seen a woman who liked to be beat," Jimmy said.

"Now that's more like it," remarked Don.

"I've seen a man inhale the fumes from a gasoline can, and that's kind of weird if you think about it," said Piper.

No one objected.

"I've seen a man shoot heroin into the vein of his neck," Don said pertly.

"I've seen a man shoot cocaine into his dick," countered Kevin, with obvious pride.

They looked to Joey.

The oldest among them at twenty-eight, Joey was the one constant in this ever changing universe. Having come to the HIPPIE HOUSE nearly a decade ago, he was the only one who could boast that he had been present at every one of the great parties over the years, which was no small feat in the others' eyes.

At six-feet-three inches and well over two hundred pounds, Joey was rather robust when speaking in terms of junkies and maintenance program alcoholics. By day he worked at Thorn's Discount Records and Tapes, and, by night, he made enough money playing lead guitar for Social Inversion to keep him in the booze, which was essential, since drinking scotch was his true full-time vocation.

"I've seen a man who couldn't stand up until he had a couple of drinks," he said, taking a swig from his giant bottle of Johnny Walker Red, which he then chased with the beer he held in his other hand.

"I've seen a man who couldn't talk until he took a hit of LSD," said Harrison, without missing a beat.

Drawing a blank, Jimmy's mind raced in a hundred directions.

"I . . . uh . . . I . . . uh," he groped before, like a bolt of lightning, it hit him. "I've seen a girl who thought she was a dog."

"I've seen people walk knee deep in concrete," Piper

65

said.

"What?" asked Joey.

"While on acid," Piper explained.

"Oh yeah. Yeah, okay."

"I've seen people melt," Don said, following suit.

"I've seen profanities spelled out in a ceiling by random cracks in the plaster," said Kevin.

"I've seen radio waves," Joey stated.

Over to Harrison.

At nineteen, Harrison was a film student at the University. A throwback Dead Head who smoked dope night and day, he had a soft spot for psychedelics and for women. He was baby-faced, kind of shy, but funny with a real off beat sense of humor. Also, he carried a video camera with him wherever he went, as if it were another appendage.

He loved to make short movies and the others all loved watching, thinking them funny. Harrison would make a tape at a party, then play it back for everyone the next day while they all sat around drinking beer and laughing at their exploits.

A couple of months earlier, however, Jimmy had let Harrison film him in a much more revealing manner than was normal for one of Harrison's classes.

Filming only Jimmy's hands and arms, he captured the entire sequence: putting it into the spoon, drawing it up in the needle, tying off and injecting. Then, for effect, he had Jimmy draw out the plunger, filling the syringe with blood, and squirt it onto the camera lens as Gang of Four's "Songs of the Free" blared in the background.

A few nights later, a young girl with a black eye and a bloody lip came wandering up to the front porch of the house wanting a beer. She had on a mini-skirt with no underwear, giving the guys beaver shots and letting her shirt slip off her shoulder, exposing her breasts, the whole time begging for something to drink - Harrison filming all the while.

Joey told the girl he would give her a beer if she danced for him and she complied.

Saying she had some money, Jimmy told her he would give her three more beers for five dollars. She gave him the money, but he only gave her one beer. When she asked for another, he told her he was out.

Next, she started talking about her job as a cheap prostitute, and Kevin told her he would give her beer in exchange for a 'blow job.' She said, "Okay," and they went inside. Upon returning the girl had a six-pack and Kevin a smile.

Superimposing this film over the footage of Jimmy shooting up, Harrison received an 'A' on his assignment.

"I've seen the spirit of a tree," was Harrison's play.

"I've seen a flower," Jimmy said, "that, if ingested, produces wild and beautiful hallucinations."

Piper frowned, stating; "I've seen a man eat a portion of a preserved cow's leg."

"I've seen the exposed tendons in a man's mutilated arm," Crazy Don chortled.

"I've seen a man drink his own urine on a dare," Kevin added.

"I've seen a man have a heart attack," Harrison said.

Suddenly, Jimmy's mind was deluged by a sea of unwelcome memories.

"Jimmy?" Someone said.

"Jimmy?"

"Earth to Jimmy?"

He looked at Joey.

"It's your turn, dude."

But his mind was on fire.

Turning to Piper, he cried, "I've got to get out of here, man!"

Standing, he ran onto the nearest beam and did not stop until he reached the other side.

"He's wiggin' out!" Crazy Don exclaimed.

Collapsing, his legs dangling over the side of The Grid, Jimmy placed his head between his hands and literally tried to squeeze out the nostalgia. It was no use.

TEN

He had just turned sixteen when his father suffered a massive heart attack.

A coal miner's son from Middlesboro, Kentucky, John Fletcher Love, Sr. grew up as poor as people get in this country and had become a self-made man, ultimately owning one of Knoxville's most successful general contracting firms until, one day, with neither warning nor portent of alarm, he was dead at the age of forty-nine.

While he remembered his father as a good man and a good parent whose drive to succeed was fueled not by selfishness, but by the desire to provide for his family all the things he had lacked growing up, Jimmy had somehow never forgiven him for dying.

Recalling how this tragedy had filled his heart with resentment, he now looked back on that time with the notion that this had been his first real experience with narcotics. Resentment being so tangible in his life that it was like a drug, intoxicating him as it secreted itself through his entire being, drowning every other emotion.

Both his mother (Helen) and Jack noticed a change in his behavior, but neither suspected that he had begun using drugs and alcohol until seven months later when, to Jack's shock and dismay, he found Jimmy lying face down on the kitchen floor in a puddle of his own urine.

Sleeping until late the next afternoon, Jimmy awoke to find his mother, Jack, and his girlfriend, Sara, at his hospital bedside. There was some small talk about how he was feeling before Helen asked him where he had obtained the pills.

He told her that he had taken them from his grandmother's bathroom cabinet. Before he died, Jack, Sr. had moved his widowed mother into a home he bought for her about five miles east of their lake house on Northshore Drive. Helen and the boys made a point of stopping by every Sunday after church.

"At Nanna's?" Helen said, surprised, rising in the chair she had pulled up beside him.

"Yeah," Jimmy said, averting his eyes.

"Why did you do it?"

His reply was blank. "I don't know."

"Do you remember how many pills you took?"

He was hesitant. "Fourteen or fifteen, I think."

"Fourteen or fifteen! You know what those pills were?"

"Painkillers."

"Were you trying to kill yourself?"

"No," he said, lifting himself into a sitting position. "Not really."

"What do you mean, not really?" Helen cried.

"I mean I wasn't trying to kill myself," said Jimmy, unsure of his motives. "I've taken them before."

"Before?"

"Yeah."

"When?"

"Lots of times."

The room fell silent. No one had suspected.

Looking at Sara, it occured to him how much she reminded him of his mother. She was beautiful, intelligent and strong and the tears in her bright green eyes stood in stark contrast to the courage of her smile, which seemed to say, 'It's okay. Don't worry. I'm here. Everything will be all right.'

The next morning he was transferred to Lakeshore

Mental Health Institute, which was to be temporary, because there were no immediate openings at any of the recovery hospitals. Two days later he was admitted to Kenesaw Hospital (one of the largest and most reputable institutions for recovering alcoholics and addicts in East Tennessee). The program at Kenesaw was tough: cold turkey from drugs, alcohol, family, friends, Sara, school, and everything else he had grown accustomed to in daily life.

Three long months passed before, at a Sunday brunch given by the hospital, he was allowed to see members of his immediate family. The patients, hundreds of them, filed into the huge dining area where fathers, sons, mothers, daughters, sisters, brothers, husbands and wives greeted them.

Happy to see his mother and Jack, Jimmy was saddened by the fact he could not see Sara and that the visit was so brief. Little more than an hour passed before the counselors and staff ushered the patients back to their routines while their families remained and were treated to a lecture on the evils of substance dependency.

After the lecture, each family was then provided an update on their loved one's progress. Helen and Jack were informed that Jimmy was doing exceptionally well and that, if his progress continued, he would be admitted into their outpatient program in two to three months. This meant he would stay in a halfway house run by the staff, attend a special school during the day as well as nightly meetings at the hospital, and be allowed to come home for an overnight visit every third weekend.

Jimmy was transferred to the halfway house exactly five months and one week after the date of his overdose. Three weeks after that, he was home for the first time in half a year.

Helen baked a chocolate cake, his favorite, and, much to his embarrassment, even bought some party favors for the occasion.

Before the festivities began, however, Jack took the opportunity to ask Jimmy the question that had been gnawing at him for months.

Flicking a loose strand of chestnut hair from his eyes as he sat across from Jimmy on the living room sofa, he said, "How did all this start, Jimmy?"

"Slowly," Jimmy answered honestly, pulling one of his legs underneath him. "You know, I never meant for any of this to happen. It just snowballed."

"You don't have to talk about it," Jack assured him.

"No, that's okay. I know you've been through a lot as well and deserve some answers."

"Well," Jack agreed, "we've all been through a lot."

After thinking a moment on where to begin, Jimmy explained, "I started off just drinking. When I'd go skateboarding over at Carl's house we would sneak a few beers out of his old man's garage. It was easy. He always kept three or four cases down there. Then one weekend when I spent the night over there, we got into his older brother's stash of pot. Carl knew right where it was and what to do with it."

"Did you guys get into pills together, too?"

"No," said Jimmy. "That was all me. I used to get some pills over there, but Carl didn't know about it. I'd act like I had to go to the bathroom and then I'd go through their cabinets. You wouldn't believe what people keep in their bathroom cabinets: uppers, downers, amphetamines, barbiturates, even hallucinogens. You name it, people got it."

"So you didn't just get 'em at Carl's and at Nanna's, huh?" asked Jack.

"Oh no," Jimmy said plainly, his voice moving up an octave. "I got 'em everywhere. All my friend's houses,

Sara's, here."

"Here?" Jack said with a start.

"Yeah. Mom keeps some pretty good stuff around here, or at least she used to. I'm sure she's gotten rid of it or hidden it all by now."

"Didn't anyone ever notice?"

"If they did, they never said anything."

"Jimmy," Jack said, rubbing the back of his neck, "why did you do it?"

"That's a good question," Jimmy thought aloud, letting his leg slide back to the floor. "I've asked myself that a million times and I'm still not sure. Maybe it had something to do with dad or maybe it was just something to do. Know what I mean? Kind of a cure for boredom, or from having to figure things out? Sometimes I wonder if there even are any reasons."

Jack nodded, pursing his lips. A long silence ensued.

"Well," Jack said at last. "Do you think you'll be able to stay off the stuff now?"

Shrugging, Jimmy exhaled a deep breath.

"I don't know," he said with a certain dark straightforwardness. "I hope so. Right now I'm sure I can, but they say that eighty percent of recovering substance abusers relapse."

"Really?" Jack was surprised.

"That's what they say."

Reaching out, Jack grabbed him by the arm, offering, "You know I'll always be here for you, don't you?"

"Yeah," Jimmy nodded. "I know you will."

"Good," he said. "Then let me say this. I know that eighty percent is a scary number, but I want you to remember one thing. It's just a statistic. That's all it is. It's not up to those eighty percent to decide whether or not you're able to keep from drinking or doing drugs. It's only up to you, little brother."

ELEVEN

"What's up? Why'd you run off like that?"

Looking up, Jimmy saw Piper's distempered frame peering down at him.

"Christ!" he breathed heavily, removing his head from his hands. "I don't know, man. I just started remembering all this shit."

"What kind of shit?" said Piper, offering a cigarette.

"Thanks," said Jimmy as Piper lit it for him as well. He took a long drag to calm himself.

"I don't know, Piper. Just all this shit that happened a long time ago."

"Well, what kind of shit?" Piper's eyes were even more penetrating than usual.

"Just bad shit, you know?"

"Hey, man," said Piper. "Don't you think that's just the acid talking?"

"Hell!" said Jimmy, scratching his head. "I know that. Don't you think I know that? It's just that . . ."

"What?" said Piper.

"It's just that I feel betrayed, that's all."

Piper smiled, condescendingly.

Jimmy felt foolish.

"Don't you ever feel like that, Piper?"

"Sure," Piper nodded. "All the time."

Both took turns drawing off their cigarettes before Jimmy continued.

"But by someone you really care about?" he said. "That's what I mean. Maybe even someone you still care about? And you kind of love them and hate them at the same time? Have you ever felt that way about anyone, Piper?"

"I'm sorry. How's that again?"

"You know, where you felt like hating someone because they let you down in some way?"

Piper shook his head. "I don't know. I don't remember."

"What do you mean you don't remember?"

"I mean not for a long time."

"How long?" Jimmy pressed.

"A long, long time," Piper said stoically.

79

"Piper, man," said Jimmy. "Did I ever tell you about my brother and my ex-girlfriend?"

"What about them?"

"That they're seeing each other now."

"The shits!" Piper guffawed unexpectedly before taking another gulp of beer. "What about them?"

"I don't know," Jimmy said thoughtfully, bowing his head. "Just that it makes you think, I guess."

"Oh yeah?"

"Yeah." He looked up at Piper. "You know, about how love and hate are so closely related?"

Taking a drag off his cigarette, Piper exhaled a large plume of smoke.

"Yeah. I know what you mean. They're hypocrites, right? They were supposed to love you, right? Be there for you, huh? Stop me if I get off track."

"No," said Jimmy, and it was as if Piper were reading his mind. "So far you're batting pretty close to a thousand."

"I've been there," Piper said. "I mean, not exactly, but close enough. How could they do that to you? That sort of thing, right?"

"I suppose," Jimmy winced, not knowing whether

80

to feel hurt or angry.

Piper threw down the stub of his cigarette and extinguished it with his boot.

"And now," he concluded, "you can't decide whether to love 'em or to hate 'em?"

Jimmy did not know what to say. Piper was right. Every word he said was as if it had been written on his forehead and read off like a cue card. Still, Piper's ability to see straight into his thoughts and emotions made him very uncomfortable.

Piper lit another cigarette and walked casually over to where he sat. Blowing out the smoke, he grinned wickedly.

"Would you like my advice on this matter?"

Not waiting for a response, he leaned down until their faces were only inches apart and, very calmly, grabbed Jimmy by the biceps.

Squeezing with all his might, he dug his nails in painfully, looked Jimmy dead in the eye, and screamed at the top of his lungs, "HATE 'EM!"

Startled, Jimmy nearly fell backward off The Grid before catching himself.

Nonchalantly, Piper stood up, took another drag off

his cigarette and said, "Enough of this shit, Jimmy! What do you say we go back to the house and break open that bottle of Cuervo Gold?"

TWELVE

"Hi," Clarissa called to the guys from the front porch of the HIPPIE HOUSE. "Where have you bad boys been? We've been waiting."

Climbing up the stairs, Piper answered, "We've just been out enjoying an early morning stroll."

"Hi," said Joey's girlfriend, Wendy, a small, pugnacious redhead, jumping up and giving him a quick kiss on the lips. "We thought the cops had come and dragged all of you down to jail."

"Oh yeah, ladies?" Don remarked jokingly, pounding the dirt off his Dingos. "Well, sorry, but you ain't got no such luck this time."

As the others continued to shuffle into the house, Jimmy spotted another petite figure, dressed in a red bandanna tank top, mini-skirt, and thigh-high boots, rocking slowly on the swing at the far end of the porch.

"Hello," Melanie said, looking up at him with her

large, unaffected blue eyes. "I was just about to give up on you."

"Really?" Jimmy said, walking over and sitting down beside her. "Where have you been tonight?"

"Nowhere, really. Caroline and I went down to Hawkeye's, but it was too crowded."

"Who's Caroline?"

"My friend from work, remember?"

"Oh yeah," he said, sitting up and putting his arm around her, his mind flashing with the recollection that she had worked at her father's pharmacy that day. "Did you get anything?"

The abruptness of the question did not sit well with Melanie.

She pulled away. "Is that all you care about, Jimmy? Whether or not I got anything?"

"No," he said, furrowing his brow, feigning hurt. "Of course that's not all I care about, Mel. Forget it, okay?"

Magically, her icy disposition melted as he reached out, brushed the auburn locks from her eyes, and gave her an apologetic peck on the cheek.

"Well," she sighed, "I got something, but I don't know what it is."

"Do you mind," he asked cautiously, "if I check it out?"

Seizing her wrist, he pulled her from the swing. As they entered the house everyone except Kevin was sitting in the living room, to the right of the foyer. Piper came over and stuck a large bottle of tequila in Jimmy's hand.

"Lime and salt on the table," he said.

"What for?" Jimmy smirked, taking two large gulps.

"Come on in, you guys," called Joey. "We're trying to pry this secret out of Piper and Clarissa."

"What secret?" Melanie asked.

"They have a big surprise in store for everyone at the party tomorrow night," answered Wendy, "and they won't tell anyone what it is."

"So," said Jimmy, looking at Piper, "what is it?"

"It's monumental," Piper said with surreptitious glee. "That's all I'll tell you. You've never seen anything like it. It's colossal. Never been tried before in the history of the universe."

"What is it?" cried Crazy Don.

"Just show up tomorrow night." Piper grabbed the bottle from Jimmy's hand and walked back into the living room. "Aren't you going to join us?"

"In a minute," Jimmy said, leading Melanie up the staircase to the second floor.

Kevin was exiting the bathroom just as they arrived. Pulling Melanie inside, Jimmy locked the door and kissed her quickly on the mouth before backing away in expectation. Noting his impatience, Melanie reluctantly opened her purse and handed him a small white pill bottle, which he wasted no time opening. Dumping the contents into his hand, he spread the nine pills out on the counter next to the sink. He was confused. Melanie's job had been keeping him on a steady diet of valiums, Quaaludes, and assorted painkillers, but these pills were unfamiliar.

"What are they?" he asked in frustration, pawing over them.

"I told you I don't know. All I know is that they're Schedule Two, which means it's a major felony to even possess them without a prescription, much less steal them."

"So you have no idea what they do?"

"No," she said, reaching down and separating the five smaller tablets from the four larger ones. "These five are called K-2's and these four are called K-4's, whatever that means."

Thunderstruck, for a moment Jimmy literally for

86

got how to breathe.

"What did you say?" he finally choked out.

"I said that these are called K-2's and these are called K-4's."

"Dilaudid," he thought ecstatically. "Synthetic Heroin!"

"Why?" Melanie said, seeing the strange expression on his face. "Do those numbers mean something to you?"

"Do they mean something?" he thought to himself. "Is that a joke? You bet your pretty little ass they mean something. They mean that I won't have to jones for coke the next couple of days."

"What is it?" she asked.

Turning away, he tried to decide what to say. He could not tell her the truth because she did not like it when he did smack. But she just did not understand. From his point of view these pills were like a miracle. Even Mr. Jones couldn't get to him once he shot one of these.

"Dilaudid," he said at last, playing upon her naïvety. "Yeah. I know what this is. It's a real downer. They use it on hyperactive kids and stuff."

"Really?" she sighed dejectedly.

Attempting to console her, he reached out and

touched her sullen lips. "I think Kevin and Crazy Don are into this kind of stuff if you want me to unload it for you."

Extremely disappointed, she pouted, "I guess so, if you don't want it."

"What's the matter?" he asked her as she shied away.

"I just want to make you happy," she said, looking at the pills on the counter.

Lifting her head he kissed her, whispering, "Don't be silly, Mel. I'm not disappointed."

He kissed her again, more deeply. And again. Without another word he put his arms around her waist and lifted her onto the counter. Moving his hand beneath her blouse, she wrapped her arms loosely around his shoulders. He leaned her back against the mirrored wall, and pulled her legs gently around his waist. Looking deep into her eyes, he ran his hands slowly up her smooth thighs, beneath her mini-skirt, where he began to tug at her panties. Reciprocating, she grabbed at his crotch, unbuttoned his jeans, and after an awkward moment, pulled him inside. They made love slowly at first.

"Tell me," Jimmy said.

"Tell you what?"

"Tell me what you would do for me."

"I would do anything for you," she moaned.

They started to make love faster. Clasping his hand around the base of her neck, he squeezed. She put her hand to his and, gasping, played at trying to pull it away.

"Oh God!" she cried. "Yes!"

Rudely, there was an obnoxious pounding at the door. He tried to ignore it, but there it was again.

"Go away!" he shouted.

"Don't stop!" demanded Melanie.

There was more knocking, even more imposing. Picking up a can of shaving cream from behind Melanie, he hurled it at the door.

"I said, Go away, goddamnit!"

"Don't stop!" Melanie commanded once more, digging her nails into his back. "Oh yes! Oh God! Ohhhh yes!" she screamed, and excited by her sexual rapture, he, too, climaxed as she collapsed breathlessly into his arms.

Once again, the pounding at the door.

"All right. All right. We're coming," Jimmy snapped.

"Sounds to me like you already came," Crazy Don laughed scurrilously from the other side.

Embarrassed, Melanie picked her panties off the linoleum and put them on hastily.

"Come on," she said as Jimmy moved to the other side of the counter, reaching down and stuffing the pills back into their bottle. Snapping the lid on he put the bottle in his shirt pocket, pulled up his jeans, and turned to her at the door.

Unlocking it, they exited as Crazy Don pushed his way past.

"Hope you all had fun in there," he commented obnoxiously. "I'm about to bust a kidney."

"Yeah," Jimmy said with tremendous disdain. "Fuck off, Don! Your tired, macho bullshit sense of humor is really starting to wear on my nerves."

Returning downstairs, they found the party thinning out. The only ones left in the living room were Piper and Clarissa, seated on the couch, and Joey in the chair opposite them.

They sat down on the floor. Everyone was growing tired and they chatted for only a couple more minutes before Piper gulped down the last of the Cuervo and declared, "Clarissa and I have to get home to the kids."

He was referring to the rats.

"How many of those things you got now?" Joey asked.

"Oh, I don't know," Piper said whimsically. "Ninety-five? A hundred? We should count, Clarissa."

"Tomorrow," said Clarissa, standing. "It's four o'clock and I'm going to bed."

"Yeah," said Joey as they all followed Piper and Clarissa to the front door. "We've got an all-nighter tomorrow night. How many people you think'll show?"

"A lot," Piper gleamed. "We've been advertising this end of the summer blow-out for a month and besides," he winked at Jimmy, "I'm sure no one will want to miss what I have in store for them."

"You sure you won't give us a hint, Piper?"

"Well, Joe, let's just say that you're in for somewhat of a supernatural history lesson."

With this elusive answer, Piper and Clarissa made their exit. As Joey retired to his room, Melanie and Jimmy made their way to the attic where they took off their clothes and collapsed into bed.

Despite the lateness of the hour, Jimmy lay wide-awake, alone with his thoughts, in the dark and stillness of the night. This, for him, was the worst time of day for he knew that the demons would soon be upon him. Like a slow pang of hunger from deep inside he could feel the jones getting stronger. Catching himself looking out the window at the clock, seeing it flash FANB - 4:17 - 74°, he thought back to a night just two weeks earlier.

Lying in bed one evening, he was struggling to fall asleep when Kevin popped up and proclaimed, "I just scored some great coke, man!"

It had been a bad day. He had gotten into a fight with his manager at work who had accused him of stealing from the register, and subsequently he had argued with Melanie. So, zombie-like, he followed Kevin to the Sunroom where they tried, as always, to string out the coke for as long as possible.

It was approaching midnight when his last turn came and he was so bent out of shape that he emptied the plunger into a muscle in his arm by mistake, missing his vein completely. His disappointment was unimaginable.

As perverse as it may seem, he knew that he had never felt worse in his life, not even when he had learned of his father's death.

Having to sit there and watch Kevin shoot the last bit of coke was unbearable. It was excruciating to see the wave of warm intoxication splash over his face, not knowing when he would feel that exquisite rush once again.

Returning to his room he laid down and began watching the clock flicker, in turn: FANB -12:47 - 66° - FANB - 12:48 - 66° - FANB - 12:48 - 66° - FANB - 12:48 - 65° - FANB - 12:48 - 65° - FANB - 12:48 - 65° - FANB - 12:48 - 65° - FANB - 12:48 -65° - FANB - 12:49 - 65°. There are no words for this misery.

The clock read 6:47 and he felt no better than he had at two o'clock. The sun was beginning to cut its way through the early morning mist and the thought of facing the day was overwhelming.

7:30 came and went and, still hours before the first signs of life would stir at the HIPPIE HOUSE, he was alone in his agony. At 8:15, his head besieged with incessant pounding and his body covered with a film of dried sweat, he sprang to his feet.

Climbing down the ladder he made his way to the Sunroom. Pushing the door open he saw Kevin, out cold in his bed. Spying a syringe in his trashcan, Jimmy grabbed it and walked out.

"An air bubble," he thought. "It'll be quick. It'll get to my heart or my brain and that will be it. Not too painful and altogether appropriate."

Needle in hand he climbed back up to the attic, sat

93

down on his bed, and looked out the window. The sun was higher now.

8:22 . . . 8:23 . . . 8:24.

Tears streaming down his cheeks, he pulled out the plunger, filling the tube with oxygen.

8:25 . . . 8:26 . . . 8:27. . . 8:28.

He made a fist and found a vein.

8:29 . . . 8:30 . . . 8:31.

Sticking himself, he closed his eyes.

8:32 . . . 8:33.

He pushed the plunger in slowly.

8:34 . . . 8:35 . . . 8:36.

Nothing.

8:37 . . . 8:38.

He filled the syringe with air once more.

8:39 . . . 8:40.

Injecting himself again, he felt a sharp pain in his temple.

"This is it!" he thought.

Frightened, he tried to stand, but became intensely dizzy. He collapsed to the floor.

12:47 - 86° - FANB - 12:47.

The first thing he saw when he came to was that

goddamned clock!

"Fuck that!" he exclaimed, throwing back the covers.

"What's wrong?" Melanie muttered.

"Nothing," he said coldly. "Go back to sleep."

Heading for the attic door, he stopped to put on his jeans before climbing down to the second floor landing. Walking down the hall, he opened the door to the Sunroom.

"What?" Kevin stirred from his bed. "Who is it?"

"It's just me," Jimmy said as his eyes adjusted, spotting the two needles they had used earlier on Kevin's desk. "I left something in here. Go back to sleep."

Picking up one of the syringes he turned and walked out, closing the door behind him. Heading down the staircase to the first floor, he found a spoon in the kitchen before returning upstairs.

Locking himself in the bathroom, he took out a K-4 (twice as potent as a K-2), dumped it into the spoon, heated it, drew up, tied off, and injected. The warmth spread from his arm to his shoulder before making its way to his torso, legs, and head. Slowly, it enveloped him as he sat on the toilet waiting to get sick. His eyelids sunk and he was grateful for the peace the drug brought.

Suddenly feeling ill, he got up and purged himself into the head. Then again. There was not much to be purged: just some beer and the Cuervo he drank with Piper.

Finished, he stood, flushed the toilet, stuffed the paraphernalia under the sink, and returned to his room.

Crawling back into bed with Melanie, he thought he saw the clock flash, 5:22. Laying back down, feeling his body begin to float, he welcomed the nods, his mind flitting in and out of consciousness.

THIRTEEN

It was late the previous spring and he had gotten in over his head with the cocaine. After the aborted camping trip, he had begun doing coke so heavily that even Kevin started worrying about him. Whereas it was old hat to him, Jimmy was new at dealing with the pull and had no idea how to handle it.

One night after Kevin and he had run out of both coke and money, Jimmy wound up in the middle of a fight at Quarter's on Seventeenth Street. From there he went to jail and it was one of the most miserable experiences of his life.

The city lock-up was always overcrowded, but this time it was particularly so. And his stay was an extended one. Normally, he would stay until morning, see the judge, and go home. This time he went in on a Friday night and it just so happened to be Memorial Day weekend, so court would not be in session until the following Tuesday.

Crammed into a filthy 40' x 60' cell with fifty to sixty other misfits and with no floor space on which to sleep, he soon began jonesing for coke so badly that he felt as if he wanted to die.

When they brought Piper in on Monday night, it was as if his savior had arrived. Seeing him, Jimmy's face lit up. Stumbling over the passed out and sleeping residents of the drunk tank, he proceeded to throw his arms around Piper, giving him a tremendous, spine-crackling bear hug (not exactly proper behavior between two men in those surroundings).

They talked all night. Piper explained that he had been picked up for disturbing the peace after getting into a fight with Clarissa. When finally released the next morning, they walked back to the house together. Upon entering the neighborhood, however, Jimmy began to feel the pull of the cocaine once more. Soon it was so strong that he knew something drastic had to be done.

His Uncle Fred was his father's younger brother, who lived in Columbus, Ohio. Jimmy walked down to GENE'S and called him collect (there was no phone at the HIPPIE HOUSE). Explaining that he was feeling very badly and that he would like very much to come see his uncle,

Fred wired him the money.

Jack and Jimmy had spent weeks at a time there as children and had always been welcomed. Fred and his wife, Elizabeth, were very likable people and they had twin boys, Steve and Vince (a year and a half older than Jimmy - exactly between the ages of him and Jack), with whom he had always gotten along.

"Once I'm in Columbus and away from the HIPPIE HOUSE," he told himself, "everything will be all right."

He knew that if he cleaned up, he could stay with Fred and Elizabeth for months. So, without telling anyone anything (knowing that if Kevin found out he had any cash that they would end up at the coke man's house and he could kiss Columbus goodbye), he hiked down to the Greyhound Station.

With all the stops, the seven hour trip took twelve and a half. Arriving at eight o'clock the next morning, it dawned on him that he had not had a drink or taken a drug since before he went to jail the previous Friday and it was now Wednesday morning.

Uncle Fred picked him up and took him to his house, located in a middle-class neighborhood just north of the city, where Elizabeth repeatedly remarked how thin and pale Jimmy looked before proceeding to cook him a hot breakfast. Vince and Steve were home for dinner that evening. Vince had a job at a local Kroger's and Steve was working part-time waiting tables while attending Ohio State.

It was a happy reunion. After reminiscing around the dinner table, Fred told everyone that Jimmy would be staying as long as he liked and Jimmy was so gratefully moved by the occasion (by just being back in a normal home, with caring people) that he actually had to fight back tears.

The honeymoon did not last long, however.

The next day Vince drove Jimmy around town, trying to help him find a job. They were just about to give up for the day when he convinced Jimmy to apply at a small package store located in the same strip mall as his grocery. As fate would have it, they hired him on the spot.

Then, Friday night, Steve asked Jimmy to go to the movies, but they were no sooner out of the driveway when Steve, the All-American boy, reached up to his visor and produced a marijuana joint a half-inch thick. Jimmy was shocked.

Lighting the joint, Steve offered it to Jimmy. Summoning all his strength he somehow managed to refuse at first. Being sober nearly a week, he was beginning to feel immensely proud of himself. But as the sweet odor of the pot began to permeate the car, he caught himself looking at the clock on Steve's dashboard. Taking evasive action, he rolled down the window.

But it was no use. Estimating that the last drink he had had was at approximately 11:15 p.m. the previous Friday, he frowned. Convinced he would never make it an entire week, he reached over, removed the joint from Steve's fingers, and took a long, satisfying drag.

Although its population is around one million, Jimmy felt there was something very small-town about Columbus. Though half its size, Knoxville seemed just as large to him, perhaps because both cities are college towns and have substantial counter-cultures. Wasting little time, he made himself a part of the scene in and around the campus of Ohio State.

By the end of that first week the home scene at Fred's and Elizabeth's had begun to bore him. Certain things were expected of him there and the kind of freedom and spontaneity he had grown accustomed to in The Fort was frowned upon. But he began to love his new job. After the initial week of training, he was left alone with all that liquor and took it upon himself to become a connoisseur.

He did manage to keep his mind off cocaine (more or less) those first couple of weeks, mostly because he did not have any money or know anyone who had coke. But his third weekend in Columbus, Steve took him to a friend's apartment on High Street (the name of which seemed ironic to Jimmy), and spotting a box of syringes on top of a chest of drawers, the demons came roaring back.

Taking Steve aside Jimmy told him that he wanted to buy a gram of coke the following Friday.

The entire next week the thought of cocaine consumed him, and when payday finally arrived he gave the money to Steve, who procured the drug. Shooting every bit that night, Mr. Jones was back in force.

While getting alcohol was no problem, coke was different. Needing far more money than he was making, Jimmy began stealing.

He would take change from Steve and Vince, go through Fred's pockets and Elizabeth's purse, overcharge customers at the package store, steal premium bottles and sell them privately, rationalizing all the while that the cocaine was responsible for his behavior.

"Coke did that," he would say to himself, and when

that did not work he would drink to forget.

But it was a vicious cycle because when he would get drunk, he inevitably started thinking about coke again. And then, to get more, he would steal.

Living a double life, he managed to keep this darker side of his character hidden while in the house, but when away from Fred's and Elizabeth's, he was as different as Jekyll from Hyde.

He was becoming more and more obnoxious when it came to partying, not to mention the fact that he could go through his own paycheck and part of Steve's during the course of a single night and still not have his fill.

Due to his experiences in Tennessee, he began to feel superior to the people he met in Columbus. No one could keep up with him, or so he thought. And he did not mind saying this to anyone who would listen.

Consequently, he estranged himself from everyone he had met until he started to feel like some sort of alien, marooned on a distant, unfamiliar planet. And this caused him to yearn for home, for Fort Sanders, and, yes, even for the HIPPIE HOUSE.

One morning, without telling anyone, he packed his stuff into a garbage bag and walked the quarter-mile to the interstate, hitching a ride to Cincinnati where a trucker (heading down I-75 to Florida) agreed to take him as far as Knoxville. The whole way back he kept thinking about how futile his escape to Ohio had been, pondering the question of whether he had carried his demons there with him or if he had simply found that those demons were everywhere.

He felt bad for his aunt and uncle, who had shown him such kindness, and knew that they did not deserve his leaving without so much as a thank you or goodbye. But he rationalized this behavior by telling himself that he would have only hurt them more by staying.

Having been gone six weeks, he walked back through the door of the HIPPIE HOUSE a defeated man. None of the guys had seen or heard from him since before he had left, and he was sure that they must have been worried about his whereabouts. He saw Joey first, watching television in the living room.

"Well, well, well," Joey said, barely looking up, "look who it is. You owe me a month's rent."

A couple of weeks later he met Melanie. There was a group of people, many of whom he did not know, gathered on the front porch, tripping on acid. Noticing a very pretty creature standing alone in the corner, he approached and asked her name.

"Melanie," she said, glancing up at him with a tense and extremely vulnerable look.

"What's wrong?" Jimmy inquired.

"I'm scared," she explained. "This is the first time I've done acid and I feel really strange."

He smiled. "Don't be frightened. Your defenses are down, that's all. Maybe you're scared because you're beginning to see things in a completely new way?"

"Yeah," she nodded. "How did you know?"

"Listen, it's okay. There's no need to be afraid. You're safe here. Just relax. I know it can be scary when what's real suddenly becomes unreal, but you know what?"

"What?"

"The shamans used psychedelic drugs to see into the realm of the spirits. They believed the essence of all things is revealed while tripping."

Melanie smiled, impressed.

Having tripped so many times, Jimmy felt he knew precisely what to say to comfort her.

"Tripping," he said expertly, "is an art form. There's a right way and a wrong way. Once you know what to expect, well, you can manipulate it. But when you're new at it, your perceptions are thrown so far out of whack that it's only natural to be a little scared."

"Yeah," she said. "I guess so."

"Believe me, I know what you're feeling. You've started seeing everything differently and your previous perceptions are breaking off, flying away one by one. You feel like you're nowhere and that's frightening. But, really, don't be scared. You're just becoming in tune with everything. That's all. Just let all your preconceived ideas go and you'll begin to realize just how perfect everything really is."

"Really?" she sighed, pushing up against him.

That night Jimmy slept at her apartment on Eleventh Street and that is when their relationship began. At first it was not exclusive. He was also seeing Karen, a waitress at Tomato Head - a pizza place on Market Square where he had recently taken a job washing dishes - who turned out to be psychotic. After a few nights, she told him she had been raised by a pack of dogs, and, truly she believed it. Later he found out that she really was certifiable and had the papers to prove it.

Also he had a series of one-night stands: one with an art student who demanded to sketch his penis before she would have sex with him and another with a girl who wanted him to burn her tits with his cigarette.

Growing tired of all the crazy, unpredictable nympho-types who hung around the house, his relationship with Melanie began getting more serious. She was really sweet, he thought. Of course, the fact that her father owned a pharmacy did not hurt either.

FOURTEEN

It was late morning and he was trying desperately to shade his eyes from the light streaming through the window.

"Are you going to be here tonight?" Melanie asked.

He could tell that she was preparing to leave by the way she was thrashing about the room. He thought if he remained motionless and silent, she would not disturb him further. He was wrong.

She shook him vigorously.

"Jimmy," she said. "I have to get going. I have to go to work."

Rolling over, he exclaimed, "Jesus! Why do you have to wake me up to tell me that? I could have figured it out by myself, you know?"

"Are you going to be here tonight?" she asked again, reaching out to brush the sleep from his eyes.

Struggling to sit up, he replied, "Where else would

108

I be?"

Melanie's body shielded him from the sun.

"What time is it?" he grumbled.

She moved aside. Squinting, he saw the clock flash: 89° - FANB - 11:26. The light was eclipsed once more as she leaned forward and gave him a quick kiss on the lips.

"I'll see you tonight," she said, buttoning her blouse and moving off hastily.

"Huh?" he said. "Yeah. Tonight. See ya."

Getting up, he put on his favorite shirt (a bleached denim button-down), which he did not bother to tuck into his jeans. From below he heard the pulsating rhythms which he knew were originating from Joey's Motorola stereo system on the first floor. David Bowie and the leftover taste of tequila were the call of the morning.

"Jesus! My brain!" he thought, clasping his forehead.

Struggling to move toward the door, the floor shifted from horizontal to vertical and in a split second, the wall kissed the side of his head with a nauseating thud. Doubling over, there was nothing in his stomach to vomit.

"Beer," he thought, steadying himself. "Must have beer."

With great effort he stood upright, staggered to the

109

hatch, and crept down the ladder. Making his way to the staircase, his mouth tasted like undried cement. Bracing himself against the railing, he attempted to focus on the task at hand. After a moment, he began to descend, trying not to step on too many of the little armored creatures indigenous to this old house as they scurried across the steps.

Wondering why cockroaches were not strictly nocturnal animals in the HIPPIE HOUSE, the music grew louder and, aided by the alcohol and smoke-stained walls, he staggered on. Suddenly, his head seared with the pain that accompanied the bright light exploding through the open front door.

The smell of oxygen mixed with the lingering alcohol and marijuana fumes so that the air was simultaneously sweet, sour, and stale. Toddling through the living room to the door of Joey's room, he bolstered himself and knocked. Listening, he heard the familiar sound of Joey's six-inch-heeled, imitation leopard skin boots (very methodical in their dull rhythm), approaching from the other side. The door opened.

The hulk of a drunk sang the chorus of "Young Americans" in his face in synch with the record on his BSR turntable, which was state of the art fifteen years ago. 'Lucifer', as Joey's alter ego was known, looked just as though he had been transported straight out of 1973, with his yellow and black spotted stacks, cowboy hat covered with pink sequins, Levi's that really were from 1973, and a plain white T-shirt, complete with rolled up sleeves.

"My savior!" was Jimmy's trembling exclamation, noting the tumbler of ice and Johnny Walker Red in Joey's left hand.

"Well, well, well," Lucifer said with his trademark smirk. "Look what the goddamned cat dragged in."

Wading through the assortment of guitars, chords, and amplifiers, which lined the room, Jimmy asked, "Do you have nectar?"

Smiling, Joey bargained, "Do you have cigarettes?"

Instinctively, Jimmy reached to his breast pocket but discovered that his pack was empty.

"No," he said, "but come on, Joe. Have a heart, will you? I'll go get some. I just need something that will straighten my gait first."

Without changing his expression, Joey turned and shuffled off to the opposite corner of the room where he reached into the large cooler at his bedside, producing a six-pack of Busch. He tossed it to Jimmy.

"We drank all the Buds last night," he muttered, "and they're warm. All the ice has melted."

"That's cool," said Jimmy, sitting down on one of the amps.

Tearing off a beer, he popped it open and guzzled it.

Walking across the discolored hardwood floor, Lucifer turned down the stereo, pulled the chair from his desk, and sat opposite him.

"Thanks," Jimmy said, discarding the first can into Joey's wastebasket.

He tore off another and proceeded to shoot it.

"Sure," Joey said, "but I want to know every detail."

Looking at him blankly, Jimmy wiped the last drop from the second can off his chin.

"What are you talking about?" he asked, crushing the can and punctuating the question with a belch.

"Last weekend," explained Lucifer. "That fine young love kitten you were licking on when we played down at Planet Earth. You got inside that thing, didn't you?"

His grin widened in anticipation of Jimmy's answer.

Opening a third can, Jimmy drank it while considering the question.

"Well," Joey said impatiently, "did you get up in her or not?"

"Which girl are you talking about, Joe?"

"You know who I mean."

Jimmy's mind had just begun to function again and he concentrated.

"Oh," he said, nodding, "you mean the brunette with the big . . ."

"Yes, her. The one with the perfect ass."

Concentrating still harder, Jimmy reached for a fourth beer.

"I don't know," he said finally. "I don't guess so."

After looking him over a moment, Joey eased back in his chair as if determining that Jimmy had no reason to lie to him about this.

"Nah," he said. "You would remember if you had gone up in that little thing. No matter how drunk you were."

"Yeah," Jimmy agreed, though he seriously doubted it.

It would not have been the first time he had drawn a blank after a hard night's drinking.

"Well," Joey said, "what's her name?"

Jimmy was positive he knew the answer. He had

gone to high school with this girl before dropping out. The harder he tried to remember, however, the more he drew a blank.

"Damn," he said in defeat. "I don't know."

"Yep," Lucifer laughed fiendishly, rising from his chair. "First signs of wet brain. Welcome to the ranks of the chronics, my man. Maybe you should go on the wagon, huh?"

"Tomorrow," Jimmy replied facetiously, replacing Joey in his seat.

Picking his electric guitar off its stand Joey sat down on the bed and, without plugging it in, began strumming a few chords. He played along with the song "Rebel, Rebel" for a time before looking up.

"Man!" he bemoaned. "If I could just join a band in Nashville or Atlanta, I know I could get paid."

"But you're in a band here, Joe. And you get paid."

Frowning, Joey looked down at his guitar and began to play once more.

The mood had suddenly shifted and Jimmy felt uneasy, perhaps because he could read Joey's mind. Unlike the other members of his band, Joey was gifted musically and smart enough to know that Social Inversion would never make it out of Knoxville.

Having a natural gift for all string instruments, he worked hard at his craft several hours each day. He also had a talent no one can either teach or be taught (playing by ear). Joey could duplicate virtually any sound made on a string instrument after hearing it only once. He could play it back chord for chord, note for note, regardless of how difficult.

The rest of Social Inversion: Greg Nixon - the bass player, Mark Gallagher - the drummer and especially Piper, were much more concerned with image than with quality. This was primarily due to the fact that the groups' drinking hours, much like a sixty-five-hour-a-week job, conflicted with any other activities in which they might like to participate (namely band practice).

Meanwhile, whatever potential Joey might have had to develop his talent, and his life for that matter, was being stifled by this environment and by his own unquenchable desire for alcohol.

It had been seven years since Social Inversion played their first show at a bar on Cumberland Avenue called The Place. Although Jimmy was not around then he had gath- ered from the others that the band was marginally well received by the alternative crowd, which longed for something different, something wild. Anything that would break up the ennui of life in Knoxville, Tennessee.

The group was a true throwback to the days of hardcore Punk. They played seven original songs that night and an assortment of Black Flag, Dead Kennedy's and Sex Pistols covers. Seven years later the band could boast of having thirteen original numbers in their repertoire.

Perhaps Joey had not been smart with his talent, but part of Jimmy respected him for his loyalty to his band mates and also for his amazing endurance. Lucifer's incredible stamina was legendary and it permeated every facet of his life: the band, his survival in the Fort, his ability to get up and go to work every day regardless of the severity of his hangover, and especially his drinking.

In terms of volume he was easily the heaviest drinker Jimmy had ever met. Day or night, Joey could be found with his bottle of scotch.

One of his favorite sayings was, "If you can't get up and go to work with the big dogs, don't stay up till the break of dawn drinking with the big dogs."

Jimmy's heart felt heavy as he watched Joey play along with the record.

116

'If I could just join a band in Nashville or Atlanta I know I could get paid.'

His words were still hanging there and Jimmy felt compelled to say something else, to offer some other, better words of encouragement.

Finally, he groaned, "You'll get your day in the sun yet, Joe."

Looking up slowly from his guitar, Lucifer smiled.

"Probably not," he said dryly, reaching out for the tumbler of scotch on his nightstand. "In ten years I'll probably be in this same house, drinking scotch out of this same glass."

Jimmy did not know what else to say.

"Aw hell, Joey," he finally laughed awkwardly, in an attempt to lighten the mood, "you'll be drinking vodka by then."

Their eyes met, and for an instant, Jimmy did not know if he had said the right thing. But when Joey chuckled, they both shared a good derisive laugh at themselves.

"Is Harrison here?" Jimmy asked, if for no other reason than to change the subject.

"Probably," said Lucifer. "I saw that little nursing student of his come in last night after you guys went to bed."

Standing, Jimmy moved toward the door.

"Listen," he said, turning around, "you mind if I drink these last two on the run?"

"Feel better?"

"I can walk now."

Jimmy opened the door and walked out. Before closing it behind him, he saw Joey belt down a half-glass of scotch without flinching.

"Bring me some cigarettes when you come back," the hulk called after him. "And some beer. You've depleted my emergency supply."

FIFTEEN

Pleased that the four beers had eased the pain in his head, not to mention that they had steadied his walk, Jimmy opened the fifth can and ascended the staircase to the second floor. Making his way down the hall, the sweet aroma of burning marijuana began to fill his nostrils. Sensing that Harrison was in the midst of his morning ritual, he knocked.

"Whoooo is it?" a mock, high-pitched voice cried out from within.

"It's Floyd the Barber," he said, in recognition of Harrison's affinity for the Andy Griffith Show.

The door opened and an immense cloud of smoke rolled out. The pleasantly stoned look on Harrison's face assured Jimmy that he had been at it for quite some time.

"You seen Aunt Bee?" asked Jimmy, pushing his way into the room. "I know she's in here. I just heard her."

Inside there was, as usual, a cute girl. She was sprawled out like a lazy cat on the mattress, which served as

Harrison's bed.

Looking at Jimmy with glazed eyes, she purred, "Hi. Wanna get stoned?"

Against his better judgment, he agreed. Although he loved to smoke dope, he was prone to attacks of dizziness when he smoked while drinking.

Harrison passed the pipe. Looking across the cubicle, Jimmy spotted the camcorder propped atop a tri-pod, aimed downward, directly at the mattress.

"Did you guys make a movie last night?" Jimmy asked the girl, exhaling.

Looking at Harrison, she did not answer. Jimmy took another, deeper hit, and involuntarily, his lungs disgorged the smoke in a ferocious coughing fit.

"Ha, Ha, Ha, Ha, Ha!" Harrison really did laugh like that.

Wiping the tears from his eyes, Jimmy passed the pipe back and took a large gulp of beer. A Roadrunner cartoon was playing on a tiny thirteen-inch black-and-white TV. Sitting next to the girl, Harrison and Jimmy watched and laughed as they passed the pipe back and forth.

After finishing off a couple of bowls, Jimmy looked across Harrison at the girl. She seemed very serene, content even, to be in this place, getting high with them.

"So," he said to her as Harrison began to load the pipe once more, "what's a nice girl like you doing in a place like this?"

The lazy cat looked at Harrison and both began giggling like school children.

"Never mind," said Jimmy, standing. "I'm headed to the Dungeon."

"Really?" Harrison said. "You don't know what this big surprise Piper has in store for us tonight is, do you?"

"No."

"Well try and find out, dude. He might tell you. I want to get it on tape for my class."

"All right," Jimmy said as he reached the door. Turning, he added, "But it's probably just something Piper thinks will impress all of his seventeen-year-old groupies."

"Yeah," Harrison laughed in agreement.

"Yeah," Jimmy laughed back, opening the door and looking back at the girl. "These young chicks seem so innocent but . . ."

"Ha, Ha, Ha, Ha, Ha! Yeah, right. Innocent. Ha, Ha, Ha, Ha, Ha!" Harrison loved the phrase, 'Yeah, right.'

"Later folks," Jimmy said, halfway into the hall.

121

"Thanks for the dope."

"Okay, dude," Harrison said, getting up to close the door. "Any time."

"Bye," the lazy cat said from the mattress.

SIXTEEN

Gene prided himself on his beer stock. Claiming to have the cheapest, coldest beer in town, he certainly had the widest selection. Beer from all over the world: Italy, Germany, France, England, Ireland, China, Japan, Jamaica, Mexico, Brazil, Canada. You name it, Gene had it, and his cooler was beckoning Jimmy.

The sun was scorching as he turned out of the shadow of the Belle Meade Apartment complex and onto Fourteenth Street where he was overcome by the overripe stench of unattended trash. Spying the two large garbage dumpsters still some distance down the hill, he crossed to the other side of the street to pass as far from the foul odor as possible. Holding his breath as he approached, he heard the clanging of aluminum cans against the pavement and immediately knew that Red and Chuck were making their daily rounds.

"Hey wild man," came a low grumble from between

the giant trashcans.

He saw the wiry, middle-aged man, clad in a third-hand pair of overalls, brushing the disheveled strawberry strands of hair from his eyes.

"Hey Red," Jimmy greeted and kept walking.

A can flew over the wall of the dumpster, crashing against the sidewalk, but the mendicant ignored it.

"Let a man get a dollar for a cup of coffee," he begged gruffly.

"Now Red," answered Jimmy, "since when do I ever have a dollar? And since when did you start drinking coffee?"

"Man's gotta eat," said the bum as Jimmy slid on past. "All I need is a dollar."

Hanging a right on Clinch Avenue, he was heartened by the sight of GENE'S, only a half-block away.

"Aw, wonderful, beautiful, lousy, stinking GENE'S. We must pay the mother's entire overhead."

Gene was straight out of New York, so it really came as no surprise that he sounded dispassionate even as he thundered forth his greeting.

"You drink too much," he bellowed from behind the counter. "You drink too early in the morning. It's gonna

124

kill you, ya schmuck."

"Good morning to you too, Gene," Jimmy said cheerfully, making a beeline to the beer cooler in the back.

Normally it would be a twelve pack of Black Label ($3.15), but today it would be something with a little more class. Since he had the Dilaudids and was therefore not in immediate need of cocaine, he would surprise Piper by bringing a twelve pack of Moretti's (Piper's favorite).

"Give me a soft pack of Marlboro Reds as well, Gene," he said, setting the beer on the counter by the register. Remembering Joey, he added, "Uh, better make that two packs."

SEVENTEEN

The Dungeon was back up the hill and two blocks east of the HIPPIE HOUSE. Smoking three cigarettes along the way, he was terribly out of breath when he arrived. He knocked and the door opened.

"This heat's a bitch, huh?" Piper laughed, motioning for him to go into the kitchen.

Jimmy noted the dinginess of the place once again. He kept assuming that Clarissa would put some effort into the interior but was beginning to realize that this was the finished product. In the months since she and Piper had moved in, all that had been done was to add a bed, two old tables (one in the living room and one in the kitchen), a couple of chairs, and a few pots and pans. The walls had not been painted or wallpapered and were exactly like those in the basement of the HIPPIE HOUSE, water-stained and cracked in several places.

Wearing black jeans, no shoes, and no shirt, Piper's

emaciated torso displayed his several tattoos. The most prominent were of a large Phoenix Rising centered above his navel, and just to the right of his left nipple, over his heart, a gothic *FTW* ('Fuck The World').

Like the rest of the apartment, the kitchen was in complete disarray. Moving some dishes aside, Jimmy set the bag on the table. Pulling out two beers, he handed one to Piper.

"Moretti's," remarked Piper, pleased. "What's the occasion?"

"I had coupons," Jimmy answered.

Selling drugs, or 'scamming' as he preferred to call it, was Jimmy's latest occupation. It was something he had fallen into after losing his job at Tomato Head (he really was the one stealing from the register).

About three weeks earlier a guy they all called the Weasel approached him, saying that he needed someone to peddle his psychedelics. This connection, plus the money he got from selling the drugs Melanie occasionally procured for him was usually enough to help him get by.

Sitting at the kitchen table Piper said that he was just about to smoke a bowl and asked Jimmy to join him. Although he knew that he was pushing his luck concerning his dizzy spells, he accepted.

Sipping his beer, he watched as Piper meticulously filled the bowl of his skull-shaped bong with pot.

"How did it go last night?" Piper asked.

"What do you mean?"

"After we left. Did you have any more trouble with the acid? Any more unwelcome memories?"

"Oh," Jimmy said, sinking in his chair, "not really."

Piper handed him the bong. Covering the chamber, he lit the bowl and took a hit. A low, gurgling sound filled the room, and when finished, he held his breath. Finally, he exhaled, handing the bong back. Everything began to move slowly and his awareness heightened. Predictably, the room began to spin counter-clockwise, slowly at first and then faster until, closing his eyes, he had to lay his head down on the table.

He heard the gurgling sound. When it stopped, Piper eked out, "Dizzy?" as he struggled to keep the smoke in his lungs as long as possible.

"Yeah," Jimmy replied weakly.

Piper repeated the gurgling.

"That's too bad," he said after a few moments. "This is some really good dope."

Opening his eyes, Jimmy raised his head.

"So?" Piper said, looking at him curiously.

"So what?"

"So are you ready to get over your brother and what's her name?"

"I don't know," answered Jimmy.

"What do you mean, you don't know?" said Piper. "Look at you now. Aren't you a lot better off?"

"Huh?" said Jimmy.

"With Melanie. I mean, it must be nice balling a babe who just happens to work at a pharmacy."

Jimmy did not say anything before Piper laughed and added, "But you know that, don't you? You're a whole lot cagier than you look, my friend."

"Melanie's cool and all," Jimmy finally answered. "But she gets under my skin sometimes. Know what I mean?"

He took a gulp of beer and his tone turned more serious.

"Piper, why do you think a girl like her will have anything to do with a guy like me? I mean, why would anyone want to put up with all the shit?"

Examining the contents of the bowl, Piper declared,

"It's fried."

Loading another, he added, "Because she's a satellite, that's why."

"What?" said Jimmy.

"You heard me, she's a satellite."

"What are you talking about?"

"You know what a satellite is, don't you? It's an object that orbits around another object, receiving signals from that object and then shooting them back. She's a satellite."

"I still don't understand."

"Look, Jimmy," said Piper. "I don't know why she puts up with you and she probably doesn't either. But that's okay. Hell, you ask ninety-nine-point-nine percent of the people in this world why they do the things they do, and they can't tell you. It's just that they're satellites, bouncing back whatever signals have been transmitted into their brains. Maybe she has an overdeveloped maternal thing going, or maybe MTV convinced her that she needed to tell her parents to fuck themselves and you seemed like the best way to accomplish that. Know what I mean?"

"I guess," said Jimmy. "It's just that she's so beautiful. And Sara? Hell! Sara was even more beautiful. I just can't understand what they could possibly see in me."

Looking up with a pained expression on his face, Piper pushed the bong at Jimmy once more.

"Here. You need this worse than I do."

The remnants of his dizzy spell having subsided, he relented. Lighting the bowl, he sucked the smoke into his lungs.

"Let me ask you something," said Piper. "Why do you care so much what other people think? I mean, it's like this brother of yours and this other girl. Why do you give a shit?"

"I just do," said Jimmy. "Don't you care about anyone at all, Piper?"

Looking up, their gazes met and, although Piper did not speak, Jimmy saw the answer in the pitch black void of his eyes.

Growing uncomfortable with the conversation, Jimmy said, "Let's smoke another bowl."

"Wait a minute," said Piper. "Don't change the subject."

"It's just not as simple as that," Jimmy snapped. "I don't want to talk about it."

"Why?" said Piper. "Is there something else?"

"Yes!" said Jimmy. "There's something else."

"Come on," Piper salivated. "I won't tell anyone. Besides who would I tell, the guys at the house? They've seen it all. If you don't know that after last night . . ."

"This is different, Piper."

"Oh yeah. How so?"

"It's just different. That's all."

"Well, you can tell me. Whatever it is."

"Okay, Piper. We had a baby together. Is that juicy enough for you?"

"Really?" Piper pursed his lips with delight. "When?"

"A couple of months before I moved into the house."

"Where's the baby now?"

Turning away, Jimmy sighed, "We had to give her up for adoption."

"Wow!" said Piper.

"Yeah," said Jimmy.

There was a pause before Piper finally said, "So?

"So what?"

"So what is the problem, now."

"The problem," said Jimmy irritably, "is that I can't

132

get her out of my head."

"Who?" said Piper.

"The baby."

"The baby? What about her?"

"Everything," said Jimmy, taking another gulp of beer. "I think about her growing up. I think about her going to school, about what she'll look like, about her having boyfriends. I think about her getting married and having kids of her own. My grandkids! I think about all the things she'll go through in her life, about all the times she'll need someone. And about how I won't be there for her."

"You can't think like that, man," Piper said.

"What do you mean I can't think like that? I do think like that."

"I mean, look at what your girlfriend did to you after she had this baby," said Piper. "She fucks you over, with your own brother no less."

"What's that got to do with anything?" said Jimmy.

"Everything," Piper said. "Are you gonna raise a kid with a bitch like that?"

Jimmy was at a loss.

"Hell, no," Piper continued. "Man, you have to forget about all that shit."

"How?" said Jimmy."

"You have to kill them."

"What?"

"In here, man," Piper tapped his chest with his finger. "You have to kill 'em in your heart."

"Why?"

"So you can live, man!"

Piper had this look on his face, which Jimmy had only seen two or three times before. It was startlingly intense.

"Let me tell you something, Jimmy," he continued, "don't be a fucking satellite. Don't be defined by some timid, bullshit morality.

"What were you gonna do, huh? Raise that kid? Go through the program again, that twelve-step circus? Hell, that's what they do to a computer, man. They program it!

"They say, 'Get with the program, mister!' But they forget to tell you that it was programs like theirs that produced hundreds of wars to get the unwilling to 'get with the program'. And that it'll be programs like theirs that'll blow this whole fucking planet to kingdom come any day now. Shit, man, haven't those fools ever heard of Babel?

"Well, fuck their program! They can destroy themselves while I watch from the sidelines."

He saluted Jimmy with his beer before downing it.

"I don't understand," said Jimmy.

Shaking his head, Piper smirked, "That's really too bad, man."

"What's too bad?" Jimmy said peevishly.

"That you can't hate. It's too bad."

EIGHTEEN

Walking back up Laurel Avenue with the rest of the Moretti's tucked under his arm, Jimmy wondered if Piper was right. Would he be better off if he could hate Sara and Jack for being together? If he could hate his father for dying? If he could hate his mother for kicking him out?

It was six weeks after the birth of his and Sara's baby when Helen trudged into his room.

"Leave me alone," Jimmy snapped from where he lay prone on his bed.

Not to be dissuaded, his mother walked deliberately toward him and, with both arms, shoved him onto the floor.

"What the . . . !" he cried as he stood.

"Shut up!" Helen shouted. "I don't want to hear it, Jimmy! You can't go on like this. You can't go on hiding from yourself with this stuff!" Reaching to the nightstand, she picked up one of a dozen or so empty beer cans and threw it forcefully into his chest.

After looking down at where the can had hit him, Jimmy looked up in amazement. This was not the kind, loving mother he knew, who was slow to anger and who never lost her temper this severely.

"But I'm eighteen and I . . . ," he began to stammer once more.

"No!" Helen yelled. "You've got to quit now! No more excuses! You hear me? Ever since the baby was born, you've been hiding. Just like with your father!" Rushing around the bed until she was standing so close that Jimmy could see the tears in her eyes, a look of resolution crossed her face. "You have to stop, Jimmy! You have to take control of your life and you have to do it now because, frankly, if you don't do it now, you probably never will."

Feeling his mouth begin to quiver like it always did just before he would start to cry, he raised his hand to his right eye and rubbed away the moisture.

"Jimmy," his mother said, pleading with him now, "you have to stop because if you don't then I can't let you stay here anymore. Do you understand? I said, Do you understand?"

Averting his eyes, he crossed to the window and looked out at the lake. It was a cold, damp winter's day. A mist was foaming over the water and, perceiving it to be rolling toward him from the far bank, his mouth stopped quivering.

"Do you understand?" his mother persisted.

Not answering, he continued staring out the window as he began to imagine the mist enveloping him like a warm, comfortable blanket, come to carry him away. He sank into it willingly.

"Jimmy? What are you doing? Are you listening to me?"

Helen was of a mind to walk over and physically shake him out of his trance-like state when, finally, he spoke.

"It's all right," he said with a deep, submissive sigh.

"What are you talking about?" said his mother, confused. "What's all right?"

But it was no use.

"It's all right," he said again, this time in a low, tranquilized whisper. "It's all right."

NINETEEN

His stomach rumbling with hunger, he determined to go back to GENE'S.

"You back again?" Gene thundered forth from behind the counter. "You gonna clean out my cooler. You gonna take all my beer. Maybe I should close my restaurant and grocery and just cater to you and your buddies?"

"I'll have the usual," Jimmy said, making his way back to the cooler.

Reaching in, he grabbed a case of Black Label and a bag of ice. Gene was still busy fixing his Turkey and Swiss when he returned. Pulling a pack of chips off a stand by the register, he opened it.

"You're not supposed to eat in here," Gene said, stuffing the sandwich in a bag and ringing up the purchase. "If you want to eat now, go into the restaurant."

Jimmy paid and left.

It was pushing eight o'clock when he got back to

the house. None of the guests had arrived, but John Tanner was there with his band, The Wine-Dregs, who were opening for Social Inversion. They were carrying their equipment in the front door when Jimmy spotted Joey behind one of the speaker stacks. Asking if he could ice down the beer in Joey's cooler, he assured Joey that he had more than enough to cover what he owed him, plus a pack of cigarettes. Grunting his consent under the weight of an amplifier, Joey told him to leave the cigarettes on his nightstand.

After dispensing all the beers save for two and the ice in the cooler, it occurred to Jimmy that he had not bathed in five days. Or was it six?

Two minutes of hot water was all one could expect at the HIPPIE HOUSE and the water turned to ice by the time he got the shampoo out of his hair. Letting out a ferocious cry, he turned off the showerhead, dried himself, put on the same clothes, lit another cigarette, opened a beer, and returned to the attic. Almost dark now, he decided he would try to nap before the party.

Unable to sleep, he soon found himself unsucessfully fighting back memories of Sara. Reaching beneath his bed, he pulled out the old white shoebox and took out a letter. Unfolding it, he began to read:

140

Dear Jimmy,

Remember the night? You know the night it happened? You had just come home from the halfway house and your mother threw that party for you. It was the first time we had seen each other in six months. SIX MONTHS!

Remember how we walked and talked for hours and then how we made love by the lake? I know it seems kind of sad and ironic now, but I'll never forget how it felt that night. It was so pefect! So right!

You know, seeing our baby girl wrapped so snug in that little yellow blanket was the sweetest thing and, yet, having to give her up was the cruelest. I know that wherever I go and whatever I do, there will always be a part of me that's missing. Is that how you feel, Jimmy?

Still, the fact is that people have two choices when their lives don't work out the way they expect or want them to. Either they can face that fact and find the strength to go on, to move forward with their lives, or else they can run or hide or blame or wallow and end up not moving forward. They go backward, instead.

I hope you know that I'll always love you Jimmy, but I just can't bear to watch you doing this to yourself anymore. And I can't go backwards!

Love Always,

Sara

Placing the letter on his nightstand, the nausea came roaring back.

Getting up, he marched to the bathroom and shot another Dilaudid.

TWENTY

He was elsewhere. Somewhere in the third world? Central America, perhaps? There was fighting in the streets. Without knowing why, soldiers were chasing and shooting at him. His leg exploded as one of the bullets caught him just below the thigh. Repeatedly, he struggled to get up but each attempt was in vain. Looking back, he saw the soldiers closing in.

There seemed to be nothing he could do. Arriving, they hovered over him like proud hunters reveling in the powerlessness of their prey. He saw their faces, his housemates: Joey, Kevin, Harrison, and Crazy Don.

Raising his pistol, Don laughed maniacally, "You didn't really think you were going to live through this, did you, boy?"

Lowering his head, Jimmy prepared to die.

Miraculously, he was saved by what seemed to be an earthquake, the ground beneath him shaking and rolling violently. Lifting his head, dust and smoke filled his lungs.

"An explosion!" he thought, coughing.

His predators were on the ground beside him, lifeless. Their bodies had provided him with a human shield.

More shots rang out. Invisible bullets swarmed past his ear. Perhaps due to an extra jolt of adrenaline, he was successful in his next attempt to stand. Hobbling toward a high-rise building at the end of the street he realized, much to his amazement, that it was the First American Bank building in downtown Knoxville. Somehow he knew what he had to do.

"I must get to the top of the building and stop the clock!" he thought, stumbling on.

Reaching the front door, he found it locked. But luck was with him as one of the bullets crashed through the glass, enabling him to open the door from the other side. Once inside, he headed down the long corridor at the end of which he found an elevator. Boarding it, he pressed the button for the top floor.

Slumping into the corner, he was startled to see a little girl with blonde hair and a yellow dress, standing opposite him.

"Who are you?" he said, frightened.

144

The girl opened her mouth as if to speak, but what escaped her lips was the high pitched cry of a baby. Screeching to a halt, the elevator doors opened and she ran out. The doors closed again before he had a chance to move.

Panic-stricken, he pushed all the buttons in an attempt to get the elevator moving again. None worked.

The elevator began to descend. First, it moved at normal speed, but it gradually began to pick up momentum.

Now he was rocketing down the shaft, once again convinced that he was about to die.

The elevator just kept falling. Long after he had expected it to crash, he was still descending. So long, in fact, that he began to wonder if it would ever hit bottom.

Abruptly, the elevator screeched to a halt.

The doors opening, he knew immediately that he was not in the building anymore. The place was very dark and standing in front of him was a hooded creature, dressed in a black cassock. He could not tell who or what the figure was, but its voice sounded hauntingly familiar as it called him by name.

"James Love," it said with authority, motioning for him to follow.

For some reason, he could not seem to resist this command.

Looking around, it was so dark that he could not see anyone else at first, but a few steps from the elevator, he noticed that there must be thousands of these hooded figures, dressed in black, all standing in line. He asked the one he was following what the line was for, but it gave no answer.

The further they walked, the more eerie he began to feel. His leg was no longer bleeding. In fact, it was as if he had never been shot at all. He grew more frightened. Had he really escaped death after all?

He ran back to the elevator as fast as he could. Boarding it, he pushed every button. But it was useless. None worked.

The figure reappeared; impatiently telling him to stop wasting time, saying that he should make it easy on himself by doing as instructed.

He ran to one of the other zombies and asked why it was waiting in line. But it gave no answer.

He ran to the next zombie, and the next, and the next. Still nothing.

Finally, he ripped one of the zombie's hoods from

its head and cried out, "What the hell is going on?"

The zombie's eyes were totally white: no pupils, no irises, just white sockets where its eyes should have been. Gaping, he just stood there while the zombie casually replaced its hood. Frantically, he went down the line asking his futile question and discovering that they all had these blindingly white eyes. Until finally, he was jolted to a stop. He had come upon a zombie he recognized.

"Sara!"

Horrified, she was just like the rest. She had the same eyes and the same catatonic demeanor. A sharp pain seared through his chest.

But something distinguished her from the others. She spoke.

"Are you The Killer of Love?" she asked.

He was numb.

Before he could start to ponder the question, the next zombie echoed, "Are you The Killer of Love?"

He tore off this zombie's hood. There, with the same eyes, the same blank expression, stood Jack.

"Are you The Killer of Love?" the two zombies repeated in unison.

"No!" he cried, aghast. "Piper is The Killer of

Love!"

Appearing next to him was the shadowy creature, who had called him by name and who had led him from the elevator. He watched in horror as it reached up and removed its hood.

"Piper!"

His eyes were black, just as they appeared in real life. Shaking his head, he laughed demonically and pointed at Jimmy.

TWENTY-ONE

Awaking, he lay in bed for a time as he often did, for there was never any pressing reason to get up unless it was to alleviate the pain of one of his addictions or to otherwise relieve his natural tensions. For the moment he felt neither to be of urgency, although he did feel a slight twinge of the desire for the white powder, which he knew would, in time, grow to be daunting and irrepressible. Reaching to his shirt pocket, he found the pills (his guardian angels) and sighed with relief.

Lighting a cigarette and looking up at the ceiling, he imagined seeing himself, the ceiling returning his stare like a mirror, cold and unfeeling. He felt comfort in this blankness and realized that he had awoken in a very peculiar state of mind which, to his amazement, bordered on contentment. Not contentment, exactly, but a certain peace that he knew was somehow connected to the Heroin-dream he had just had.

But what did it mean?

Memories of Jack and Sara, of his mother and father, of his own hypocrisy, which had been torturing him of late, now seemed remote. He was thankful for the reprieve.

At a quarter till eleven, the music having started, he made his way down to the second floor. At the end of the hallway he bumped into Doc Shock. Doc was dressed in his usual fashion; black leather Harley Davidson jacket, army pants, and standard issue combat boots. He smiled. Two of his four front teeth were missing, one of which he compensated for with a gold filling. Jimmy smiled back, rubbing Doc's shaved head.

"Hey, Doc. Long time no see."

Rubbing Jimmy's already mussed up hair in return, Doc greeted, "Jimmy, my man! What's been happening?"

"Oh, you know, Doc. I got a job, a wife and some kids, a house, a dog and, oh yeah, a white picket fence."

"What?" Doc laughed, gesturing to the smoke-filled living room below. "And gave up all this?"

Looking, Jimmy saw what appeared to be nearly a hundred guests, more diverse than the usual crowd, drinking, smoking, and apparently having a good time. Laughing, he moved on as Doc slapped him gregariously on the back.

On his way down the staircase, he stepped over a couple, who were obviously stoned. The guy was meticulously fondling the girl's breasts beneath her blouse as she, quite pretty and seemingly oblivious to his touch, looked up at Jimmy and smiled. Smiling back, he walked on.

Wading through the living room he realized he had been right. While he knew most of the people, regular members of the underground community, the crowd was more diverse than usual. Not everyone was dressed in the same slovenly unkempt, carefully careless manner. In fact, some members of this crowd were quite respectable looking; especially some of the females.

There was Becky, for instance, a twenty-eight year old flight attendant who had been to the house only once before. Jimmy remembered how she had come home with Kevin one evening and how they had turned her on to shooting coke. She had seemed innocent in many ways (smiling the whole time) and he had actually warned her, trying to talk her out of it. But she insisted.

He remembered her face as it ran through the range of emotions he knew only too well: loving it, then hating it, and finally, hating loving it.

Then there was Flowery. She was seventeen, beautiful, and for whatever reason, had the hots for Piper. A student at Catholic High School, Piper liked her to wear her plaid, parochial schoolgirl uniform to the parties. This got him off, he explained, for when he fucked Flowery, it was more than simply a defilement of her, it was a defilement of the God who either did not exist or who simply did not give a fuck. Naturally, Clarissa hated her, so they had to be discreet.

Jimmy walked on toward Joey's room. A hand on his shoulder stopped him in his tracks. Turning, he saw Jasper, a regular at the house. A twenty-year-old burnout whom Jimmy had first met during his time at Kenesaw, Jasper was notoriously fond of bodily piercings. To Jimmy's knowledge, Jasper had eight ear pierces, a nose ring, and a sterling silver tongue stud. It was even rumored that he had had his scrotum pierced.

"Jasper," he said in greeting.

"Ji . . . Ji . . . Ji . . . Jimmy," Jasper said with a grin. "How are . . . you . . . you . . . do . . . do . . . do . . . doin'?" Besides his penchant for putting holes in his body, Jasper was famous for being a walking identity crisis, never speaking without a stutter.

Jimmy frowned. Somehow Jasper always made him nervous.

"Okay," he said at last. "How are you, Jasper?"

"Well, you na . . . na . . . na . . . know, Ji . . . Ji . . . Ji . . . Jimmy. Okay, I gue . . . gue . . . gue . . . guess."

Excusing himself into Joey's room, Jimmy grabbed two beers from the cooler and exited through the kitchen to avoid Jasper. Making his way into the basement, The Wine-Dregs were in the middle of their rendition of "Mexican Radio." It was uncanny.

The thing about John Tanner was that he had a phenomenally versatile voice. He could sound just like Wall of Voodoo when he wanted and then, on the very next song, he could be the vocal spitting image of David Byrne singing "Psycho Killer" or of Angry Samoans wailing "Tuna Taco."

Finishing their set at a quarter after twelve, Jimmy followed the crowd upstairs during the interlude. Spying Joey, Kevin, and Don mingling, as well as Harrison running back and forth with his camcorder, he noticed that Piper was conspicuously absent from the scene.

After availing himself of more beer from Joey's

cooler, he headed for the front porch where he bumped into Casper, a friend of Doc Shock's. He was in the middle of telling a story to a group of bystanders.

Casper was not his real name. No one knew his real name, but it was easy to understand why everyone called him by his nickname. He was so thin, pale, and anemic, with hair ghostly white and eyes set wide apart, sunk deep into his skull, that he actually looked more dead than alive.

"Then one day last month," he said, "my coke man got me a sheet of acid and I took a hit, then a second, a third, and I even went back for a fourth. I'd never really done more than two hits before and I was wasted. I sat out on the porch, watching the clouds form and then disappear. People came and went all day long and I greeted them with an ear-to-ear grin because, although they were walking on concrete, it was like soup or pancake batter two feet deep. I thought I was losing my mind for good, but I didn't care. Hell, I thought it was funny. Then Doc's girlfriend walked up crying and it nearly freaked me out. I was just in no mood, you understand? She asked if I knew Richard Lattimore and I said, yes. Then she told me that he had shot himself in the head. He was dead. Jesus Christ!

"Well I'd been thinking about the clouds coming

154

and going, and the people coming and going, and I saw this pattern that everything was coming and going. Now, Richard had gone.

"She went on to say that they were cousins but that they were more like brother and sister. She told me about how they had played together as kids and about how he had gone bad. She'd tried to help him but he had been on the needle for years and owed big money. He'd left town with a bunch of unpaid-for drugs about nine months earlier and then he'd come back without telling anyone. Well, all I could do was pat her on the back and watch her cry 'cause I didn't know what to say.

"Then Doc came down that evening, way fucked up, telling everyone that they never knew the real Richard. It seemed that the funeral had been that day and Richard's family had not bothered to tell any of his friends. They didn't tell us because they knew we would come to the burial and that we'd have a wake for him. The kind of wake Richard would have wanted.

"Doc had this huge bottle of Paregoric, that's opium, and he kept talking about how we were going to party on Richard's grave. He said that he was going to bury a sixer of Busch and a pack of Camels with him. Then he wanted me to take him to the cemetery but I was in no mood, man. Ha! Fuck that! I was in no mood, you understand, 'cause I'd just taken another hit along with Piper and Clarissa.

"So, finally, we all just went walking and it was weird, man. It was weird because, as we walked, all of these people were coming out of their houses and walking with us. We didn't know any of them but they were all tripping, too. We found a party and crashed it. By the time we got there we must have been thirty strong, and Piper and me were getting off on how weird it all was and the whole time Doc's feeding us this opium syrup and saying that we had to get to Richard."

Hearing a small voice call his name tore Jimmy's attention from Casper.

Dressed in a white T-shirt tied off at the navel and jeans with holes in the knees, Melanie bounded up the steps to greet him.

"Hi," Jimmy said, surprised that, judging by the liveliness with which he uttered this greeting, he was actually glad to see her.

"What's going on here?" she asked, pointing to the crowd gathered around Casper.

"Oh, nothing," said Jimmy. "Just one of Casper's

ghost stories . . . Wanna beer?"

"Sure," said Mel.

Taking her by the hand he led her through the crowd to Joey's room. Removing three Black Label's from the cooler, he handed her one, stuffed one in his shirt pocket and opened the third.

"Hey," Joey said, peering in from the kitchen. "What's going on in there?"

"Just getting some of my beer," Jimmy answered.

"Oh yeah," said Joey, walking in with his bottle of scotch.

He reached into the cooler and took one for himself.

"When are you guys going to start playing?" Melanie asked, checking her watch. "It's almost one o'clock."

"We can't yet," Joey explained. "Piper and Clarissa are in the basement setting up their big surprise."

TWENTY-TWO

A few moments later, everyone finally getting the okay to enter the basement, Melanie and Jimmy loaded themselves with as much beer as they could carry and headed downstairs. Following a path cleared by Joey's immense frame, they made their way through the throng of eager guests to the front of the stage.

"Nice of you to join us, Lucifer," said Piper into his microphone at center stage. "This is Lucifer McSatan everyone," he continued, pointing at Joey plugging in his guitar as a shrill electric vibration came over the speaker, "the Johnny Walker poster child."

This was the first time Jimmy had seen Piper all night.

He was dressed in a ripped white T-shirt which read in black print, Property of I HATE U Athletic Department, his black leather jacket, black jeans and boots.

Commanding with a wave of his hand, Piper hushed

the audience and began reciting an original poem:

"I know victims of the curious disease,
The self-serving sarcoma growing on society.
The sickness and the sadness spread through fear and pain,
The insidious brand of madness and it's driving me insane
For I have heard the little lies and alibis
For dreaming little dreams of living little lives
And I've envisioned it all with these beady little eyes."

The blue light from behind the stage cast him in an eerie, pale glow. Taking a drag off his cigarette, he continued:

"I know victims of the conditioned,
Unoriginally spawning yet another repetition,
And I hate their closed minds
Almost as much as their bleeding hearts
And that is why I don't understand their kind
Or even try to bridge the gap which is keeping us apart."

"Wheww Hew!" came a cry from the crowd. "Get off, Piper!"

Several others, including Jimmy, followed suit by yelling out their support for the madman at center stage, but then, to everyone's amazement, came the cry, "Why don't you play, goddamnit? It's late!"

Defiantly, Piper continued:

"Oh I am not a monster
Nor an abomination,
Don't you understand?
I am a leper,
Some sort of mutation
And that is why I am
The Killer of Love!"

The band struck the first chords of "Homeless Jesus", an S.I. standard, and the crowd swayed forward, Melanie and Jimmy caught in the crush.

TWENTY-THREE

"We're Social Inversion," Piper cried into the microphone as the band finished their second song, "Rotten To The Core." "And we've been kicked out of every club on the strip!"

The crowd roared on cue.

"Are you having a good time?"

Everyone roared again.

"Good," said Piper with his showman's sensibility. "Because tonight is a very special night. I have a surprise for you. Tonight I'm going to unveil the best kept secret in Fort Sanders. Tonight your lives will change forever."

Pausing, it was evident that he was extremely excited by what he had planned.

"Does anyone here believe in reincarnation?" he asked.

A lone female voice cried out from the back of the room, "Yes. I do."

"Well," Piper said, glaring into the darkness, "that's good because I do, too."

Laughing, Jimmy knew that nothing could be further from the truth.

Piper continued, "Now, I want you to bear with me for just a few minutes while I relate this tale because it'll come as a revelation."

Pausing, he reached back, grabbed a large bottle of Jack Daniels from atop one of the speakers, took a swig, and returned to center stage.

"You may not know this," he continued, "but this neighborhood, Fort Sanders, is named after General William P. Sanders who served in the Union Army during the Civil War. That's right. He was shot to death by the Confederates right here on this very hill, where this house sits, and yes, right where all of you are standing right now. It's true. I swear to God.

"During the Civil War the Union Army occupied the city, fortifying this hill, and the Confederates, led by General Longstreet, marched on Knoxville in November, 1863, and killed General Sanders in the battle.

"But then, do you know what happened? That's right. The boys in blue rallied, drawing inspiration from their fallen leader, and routed those rebel boys."

The crowd stirred anxiously.

"Now," Piper said, "this was the pivotal battle in the fight for Knoxville and the Union held the city until the end of the war. In fact," he chuckled, "they still hold it, don't they?"

He wiped the sweat from his brow.

"So you ask, 'Why is he telling us this?' Well, I'll tell you why." He shouted, "Because General Sanders is back! General Sanders is back and he's alive and well and living right here in the Fort."

Turning to the side of the stage, the spotlight moving with him, he pointed to Clarissa who held in her arms a thick trunk-like object, covered with a mangy red blanket. Walking across the platform she handed it to him. Along with everyone else in the room, Jimmy wondered what was underneath.

Lifting the object above his head, Piper exclaimed, "Here is my proof that General Sanders is alive!"

Everyone fixed their eyes on the box.

"What's in there?" came a cry from beside the stage.

"Show us, Piper!" came another.

"Would anyone like to venture a guess?" Piper

teased. "Because I tell you, not only is General Sanders alive, he's among us right now, in this very room. Would anyone like to guess which one of us he is? No? Well, then, I guess I'll just have to tell you."

"Tell us, Piper!"

"Who is it?"

"Okay, okay," he said, waving his hands in front of him. "The identity of General Sanders is, or should I say the present day conductor of his immortal spirit is . . ." He smiled wickedly.

"Come on, Piper!"

"Tell us, Piper!"

"General Sanders is . . ."

"Who?"

"Me!" he said finally as Mark Gallagher crashed the cymbal on his drum kit.

"Ahhhh," the audience sighed.

"Get out of here, Piper!" someone yelled.

Clarissa threw a cowboy-style Union Cavalry officer's hat across the stage to Piper, which he placed on his head.

"It's true," he said. "I swear to God."

"Yeah, right!" someone said. It had to be Harrison.

164

"No," said Piper, lifting the mysterious covered object above his head once more. "Remember, I have proof."

A hush fell over the room.

"That's right," he added. "In here are the reincarnations of my soldiers, brave souls all."

Jimmy suddenly realized what was in the box.

"Show us, Piper."

"What's in there?"

"Yes," Piper agreed. "But first I must tell you why these soldiers have returned to serve under my command."

"Tell us."

"Because there's another war going on! A Civil War!" he exclaimed, his eyes growing more intense. "There's a Civil War going on and most people don't even know it. But the slaves must be freed!"

"Yes," Jimmy muttered to himself. "Free them, Piper."

"Where?" someone else cried.

"Between who?"

"See what I mean?" Piper thundered. "But my soldiers know. My little foot soldiers know." He tapped the box with the palm of his hand. "And they're ready to fight!

They're ready to die! For you! For me! Do you understand? It's us against them! I said, do you understand?"

"Yes!" Jimmy shouted.

His eyes met Pipers. He felt an electric shock run through his body.

"I'm talking about the streets of Paris, man," Piper continued. "I'm talking about 1870-71, twenty thousand people murdered, the streets as red with blood as with rain, and my soldiers coming out and eating at the bodies."

He was quoting from one of his favorite books, Notes of a Dirty Old Man, by Charles Bukowski.

"Now," Piper said, "they've got us out-manned and we can't fight them with conventional weapons, but don't worry because in here," he tapped the box again, "are our secret weapons."

"Come on!"

"Show us, Piper!"

"In here is the army with which we're going to free all the slaves."

"What?"

"Show us!"

Pulling the box back down to his shoulder, he walked to the stack of speakers lining the left side of the stage.

166

Placing it on top of the stack he took another gulp of whiskey and called, "Drum roll, please."

Mark Gallagher began pounding his snare as fast as he could and the rat-tat-tat-tat-tat of the drum filled the room. Piper, one hand clutching the old red blanket, stared out at the audience.

"Voila!"

The cymbal crashed once more.

"Eeeww!" came a mass groan.

"Oooohh! That's sick, Piper!" someone cried.

Jimmy laughed.

"These are the greatest soldiers on earth!" Piper cried, basking in the audience's revulsion at seeing the dozen or so furry rodents scurrying over one another in their cage. "They're the greatest soldiers because they're the last things to drown, burn, starve, and the first to find food and water because they've been doing it for centuries. The rats are the true revolutionaries; the rats are the true underground! And not just rat rats, but human rats, too!"

He was paraphrasing from Bukowski again, but few were listening now.

"Eeeww!"

"Gross!"

The audience, like the rats, were working themselves into a frenzy.

One spectator took genuine offense.

"You're sick man!" was the rather personal remark, which came from a couple of rows behind Jimmy.

"Yeah?" Piper said into his microphone. "Fuck you!"

"Fuck you, you freak!" The voice cried again, this time louder and more pointed. "Why don't you get those fucking things out of here!"

Curious to see the heckler who had the nerve to speak this way to Piper, Jimmy spotted a rather large, conservative looking guy dressed in khakis, an oxford, and penny loafers. He quickly surmised that the poor guy did not realize just how far out of his element he was.

"Hey pal," Piper said, "this is my world and you're just in it."

The room fell silent. Everyone turned their attention to the spectator, half-hoping he would keep his mouth shut and half-hoping he would say something back to see what Piper would do.

"Just get them out of here, you fucker!" the heckler suddenly demanded.

The crowd gasped. No one had ever heard Piper

challenged like this.

"I've got a better idea," said Piper, walking back to center stage.

"Oh yeah? What's that?"

Looking the guy up and down, Piper said coldly, "Why don't you get out of here, you fuck!" whereupon he leapt from the stage (completely over Jimmy and the first two rows) onto the spectator, knocking him to the ground.

Parting, the crowd watched as Piper pummeled the heckler. Wailing on him unmercifully, he took turns punching and kicking him furiously.

"Why don't you get the fuck out of here, you fucking maggot!" he shouted.

"Why"

Punch!

"don't"

Punch!

"you"

Kick!

"get"

Punch!

"the"

Kick!

169

"fuck"

Punch!

"out"

Kick!

"of"

Kick!

"here!"

Punch!

"Okay, okay," Jimmy said, grabbing Piper from behind and pulling him off the beaten man. "I think he gets the message."

"Get him out of here!" Piper said viciously.

Jimmy nodded and Piper turned back to the stage.

"Are you all right?" Jimmy asked the spectator, whose face was broken and bloodied.

Hurt and confused, the guy did not answer. Jimmy helped him to his feet. Beside the spectator now was a crying girl (evidently his girlfriend), and Jimmy suggested she take him out of there.

"I told him we shouldn't come here," she sobbed hysterically as they moved off through the crowd.

"Sorry for the interruption," Piper's voice echoed through the basement. "Now if there are no further objections, we'll get on with the show."

The band broke into "Apocalypse," a dark, brooding song inspired by Piper's days as a Theology student. Piper's angst-filled song and dance routine swept across the stage as Joey and the rest of the band belted out the music chord by chord.

Responding, the crowd turned its attention away from the rats (still in their cage atop the speaker) and the pummeled heckler to the antics on stage. Song by song the audience danced fast and furiously, slamming into one another, lifting certain members high into the air and passing them around as if a capricious wave of humanity had swelled and was carrying them to-and-fro. At one point, Jimmy was carried away and tossed around, until he was eventually returned to his spot next to Melanie in the front row.

The band was playing one of their tighter sets in recent memory. Joey was playing especially deftly, jumping and gyrating through the set. And Piper was more electric than ever. His presence as a front man was truly remarkable.

"Okay," Piper said breathlessly into the microphone. "We're going to do one more for you."

The band began to play, "Essential Dimensions."

Piper bounded into the audience where he was ceremoniously passed over the crowd like a victorious war hero, somehow still managing to sing the lyrics. Halfway through the song he was returned to the stage. Lifting his fist high into the air in recognition of his faithful following, he was rewarded with an uproarious cry of devotion.

As the song began to wind down, he made his way back to the stack of speakers, picking up the cage before returning to the microphone. Spinning around, he feigned throwing the rats onto the audience, causing everyone to gasp. Again he pretended and the audience pitched back frightfully. Finally, he turned his back and set the cage down. Everyone sighed with relief.

Just as the last chords of the song were being struck, however, he stood, cage in hand. Twirling around, jumping, swinging and convulsing wildly, he shook the rats out onto the audience.

The crowd rioted.

Screaming and clawing their way through, over, and around one another, everyone tried desperately to get to the basement stairs. Many were pushed to the ground. They were stepped over if they were lucky, stepped on if they were not.

Holding Melanie at the front of the stage, Jimmy lifted her onto the platform before climbing up himself to escape the carnage. Glancing over at Joey, whose mouth was agape in disbelief, he heard a familiar laugh from behind.

Piper was moving toward him, carrying what looked to be a mop handle. He watched with amazement as Piper reached over the panic-stricken audience with his pole. He saw a large, cylindrical object suspended from the ceiling hanging on a link chain, wrapped around one of the basement's steel support beams.

Fitting the handle through a latch in the bottom of the object, Piper pulled.

The deluge of rodents upon the spectators was sickeningly frenetic. A hundred rats were now clawing, crawling, running, and biting their way through the audience. A shrill, shrieking noise, like the high pitched squelching of tires on a rain-soaked street, began to drown out their cries.

To compound matters, Piper then crossed the stage to the breaker box on the back wall, opened it, and pulled the switch. As horrifying and appalling as the scene had been while the lights were on, it was infinitely more so now. Grabbing Jimmy's arm, Melanie clutched it so tightly that, for a moment, he thought a rat was clawing him.

It was then, in that dark, deafening instant that his change of heart began. Until that very second he had still believed in Piper, believed that he had had some reason for playing this sick joke. But this was too much.

"Turn on the lights!" he shouted angrily.

His demand was not met and the terror continued in pitch-blackness. Minutes passed, or so it seemed, and the horrific scene had grown so intolerable that he decided to take it upon himself to get the lights back on. Just as he moved off into what he thought was the direction of the breaker box he stepped off the end of the stage, chin first onto the concrete floor.

"Shit!" he cried, but the audience and rats were so loud that he did not even hear his own curse.

Rubbing his chin, he felt a gash. Blood was streaming onto his neck. Lifting himself to his knees, he felt something scurry over his shoulder and down his back. Jumping up, he shook the horrible creature off and climbed back on stage. The lights came on.

Seeing Jimmy stagger, Melanie ran to help. Glancing toward the breaker box, he saw Piper. There was a look of immense satisfaction on his face as he stood, savoring the moment.

"And the muttering grew to a grumbling," Piper quoted from Robert Browning's <u>The Pied Piper of Hamblen</u>, his eyes seemingly bright red in the new light. "And the grumbling grew to a mighty rumbling; and out of the houses the rats came tumbling. Great rats, small rats, lean rats, brawny rats, brown rats, black rats, gray rats, tawny rats!"

He threw his head back and laughed for all he was worth.

TWENTY-FOUR

The scene on the first floor looked like the aftermath of a battle. The people who had not already left were busy nursing their scrapes, bruises and bites. Making their way to the front porch, Jimmy and Melanie found the entire gang smoking cigarettes. Piper had his bourbon, Joey his scotch, and the others, a beer.

"What happened to you?" Crazy Don said, observing Jimmy's bloodied chin.

Jimmy did not answer.

"That was great!" Don exclaimed, turning back to Piper. "Fucking great!"

Stoically appreciative of the compliment, Piper nodded, taking a gulp from his bottle.

"Now I have to admit," added Kevin, "that was original."

"Fucking great! That's what it was," Crazy Don reiterated.

"Well," Piper said to Jimmy, just as he had done the night before at The Grid. "What did you think?"

Jimmy just glared at him.

"What's wrong with him, man?" Crazy Don said to the others.

"Are you okay?" Joey asked.

"What the fuck, Piper?" he finally seethed.

"What the hell are you talkin' about, boy?" Crazy Don interjected.

Ignoring him, Jimmy repeated, "What the fuck, Piper? People could've really been hurt."

"Oh, ain't that sweet?" said Don as he moved to Piper's side. "He's lookin' out for everyone, just like a little girl who's gone and got a bump on her chin."

Jimmy yelled in Don's face, "Fuck you, Don! I'm not talking to you! I'm talking to Piper!"

"Hey, what's your problem, boy?" Don yelled back.

Jimmy's hatred for this little ignorant man swelled to immense proportions.

He screamed, "I haven't got a problem!"

"Well, you're gonna have one if you don't watch out!"

Unable to restrain himself any longer, Jimmy shoved

177

Don back against the porch wall. Don reached for his gun, but both Piper and Joey grabbed him before he could get to it.

"I'll get you, boy!" he cried, struggling to free himself. "I'll get you good!"

"What?" Jimmy said, feeling no fear. "Are you going to shoot me? Is that what you're going to do?"

"You're goddamned right, boy! I'm gonna blow your brains all over the place!"

Melanie began screaming uncontrollably. Throwing her arms around Jimmy's waist, she tried to pull him away.

"Why don't you both shut the fuck up!" Piper demanded. "Nobody's gonna shoot anybody, goddamnit!" Turning to Jimmy, he said, "Listen, if you have a problem, let's hear it."

Still glaring at Don, Jimmy muttered yet again, "What the fuck, Piper?"

"What the fuck are you talking about?" Piper cried, incensed.

"You know what I'm talking about!" Jimmy exclaimed, turning to him.

"No!" Piper shouted back. "I don't know what the fuck you're talking about!"

178

"Come on, Piper!"

"What?" Piper made an innocent gesture with his arms, expelling his breath in mock laughter. "Just because I shake some people up with a few rats?"

"What's the deal, Piper?"

"What's the deal? I shake a few people up and tear them out of their precious shells and I have to explain it to you? Come on, Jimmy! You're smarter than that. What's the matter with you?"

"This isn't about me, Piper."

"Oh yeah? Then who's it about?"

"It's about you. Just who do you think you are?"

"Who am I?" Piper asked rhetorically, shaking his head. "Well, well, well. Who the fuck are you?"

Piper's question shattered him.

Was he any different from the others? He felt hopeless. Knowing that there was nothing he could say, he cried out in frustration and ran inside.

Climbing the staircase, he locked himself in the bathroom, closing the door in Melanie's face. Reaching to his breast pocket, he discovered that the pill bottle was missing.

The full consequence of the moment did not regis-

179

ter immediately. He watched himself in the mirror, unconsciously patting down his shirt pocket as if he somehow expected that God was playing a cruel joke and that the Dilaudids would re-materialize at any moment. As if suddenly struck by an invisible hammer that sent a spark of understanding shooting through his brain, he realized the magnitude of his plight.

"No!" he cried, falling to his knees.

Collapsing to his side, he curled his legs tight against his body.

Picturing himself as a ball of conflicting desires wound so tightly that it was virtually coming apart at the seams, he felt himself spiraling downward, becoming denser as he traveled, like a snowball. But this ball was not picking up snow. This ball was picking up excrement.

"Jimmy!" Melanie gasped, pounding at the door. "Are you okay?"

He did not answer. Knowing that he could not make it through the night without the pills, the thought of going on living like this was intolerable. The pills would have pacified him, anesthetized the reality, pushing it back into the half-light just long enough to get through this crisis.

He told himself that this was simply another crisis.

It was not as though he were unfamiliar with them or with what he called hitting bottom. No one knew better than he that hitting bottom was a relative thing. He had done it so many times in the past, only to discover later that there was yet another level of despair to which he had not previously sunk.

But no. He simply could not go on without the pills.

Sitting up, he extended his legs straight out in front of him and began to debate just how to end this miserable life of his when a thought flashed in his mind.

"The pill bottle!"

He remembered where he must have lost it.

Springing to his feet, he flung the door open. Startled, Melanie stepped back. He ran to the end of the hall and quickly made his way down the stairs and into the basement. Freezing at the foot of the basement stairs, he saw a lone rat in front of the stage. It was snorting at something on the floor. He recognized the object.

His heart raced. The only questions now were whether or not it had come open when he fell from the stage and, if so, would there be anything left inside? Cautiously, he approached.

The rat scampered beneath the stage. A few feet

181

from where the bottle lay, he got down on all fours. Crawling up to it, he saw that there was no cap on the end.

"God!" he thought. "Please let there be something inside."

Bringing the bottle to his face, he looked inside. He laughed bitterly.

This bottle was now the crowning symbol of his soul, he thought, for both lay face down on the filthy floor of a rat-infested basement, completely and utterly empty.

TWENTY-FIVE

"Jimmy!" Melanie cried, running down the stairs. "What are you doing? What's wrong with you?"

Kneeling, she rolled him over.

What?" she said. "Please tell me what it is?"

Somehow her compassion enraged him.

"You tell me!" he shouted. "Just what the hell are you doing here?"

"What?" she asked, confused.

"You heard me. What are you doing here?"

Standing, she did not reply.

"What are you doing here?" he yelled again as he stood. "It's a simple question!"

"Have you gone crazy?" she cried. "What's wrong with you?"

"Answer me, goddamnit!" he shrieked at the top of his lungs. "What the fuck are you doing here?"

Frightened, she stepped back.

"Because you're here," she said finally, in a violent burst of an answer.

"Then why me?" he asked.

"What do you mean, why you?"

"Is it really so difficult to answer these questions? All I want to know is, why me? What do you see in me?" Raising his voice again, he shouted, "What in the hell could you possibly see in me?"

"I don't know what you're talking about!" she gasped. "I love you."

"But why?" he persisted. "I want to know why!"

"I don't know!" she cried. "I just do! There's no why! I just love you, that's all."

"I want to know why!" he wailed, moving toward her.

"There has to be a why! Tell me why, goddamnit!"

"I don't know!" she cried, covering her head with her hands as she sunk against the wall to escape his attack.

Lifting his fist high into the air, he swung down savagely. Just missing her face, he struck the wall instead.

Screaming, Melanie ran out.

The force with which he hit the wall had broken his hand and he knew it instantly, but as he made his way up the staircase to the first floor, he scarcely noticed the pain.

The house seemed deserted now. Only the empty beer cans, liquor bottles, and cigarette stubs – the remnants of the party – remained. Zombie-like, he found himself walking out the front door.

"James Love?" a familiar voice called to him.

Piper was sitting on the swing, accompanied only by his bottle of Jack Daniels. He motioned for Jimmy to join him and, numbly, Jimmy complied. As he leaned back against the wall opposite Piper, Piper offered him the bottle. He declined.

"You're not still mad at me, are you?" Piper said, taking a drag off his cigarette.

Jimmy did not respond.

"You know, Jimmy, it's not really about shocking people," Piper continued. "It's about showing them reality. Do you know what I mean? It's important to me that you understand because even most of the people who think it's cool that we breed those things don't get it. Hell! To them it's like going to see some horror flick. It's like going to see A Nightmare on Fucking Thirteenth Street. They experience fear and revulsion. They get their adrenal glands pumped for them, but they don't have to suffer the conse-

185

quences. I mean, I actually live with those rats, man!"

Pausing to light a cigarette, he explained, "But we're not like the rest, Jimmy. We've dropped out of society. We've stopped playing by their rules. And I'll tell you another thing. That knowledge is what keeps me going. That's how I live with myself. And if you don't mind my saying so, my man, you're going to have to come to the same conclusion if you're going to survive here. You can't be ambivalent. You have to make up your mind. Don't be like the others. The hypocrites. The slaves! It takes balls to tell society to go fuck itself. It takes balls to say, Hey Fuck you, society! Look at me! Look at us! We're living proof that if you drop out then you'll end up here."

Throwing his arms into the air, he asked eagerly, "And do you know where here is, Jimmy?"

"Yeah, Piper," Jimmy said. "I know where here is."

"Oh yeah," Piper said, grinning. "Where?"

"Nowhere."

"Shit!" Piper exclaimed. "There you go again."

"Well, tell me then," said Jimmy. "Just where is here, Piper?"

"Here is reality," said Piper, gesturing up at the house. "This place is reality. The ugly, filthy, vile reality of the world. And we are ass deep in it, my friend."

Jimmy was in no mood to argue. Pushing himself off the wall, he started down the stairs to the sidewalk.

"Hey, wait a minute," Piper called after him. "Where are you going?"

He turned back.

"If this is reality, Piper. I don't want any part of it," he said.

He started towards the street once more, but Piper would not relent.

"Why do you drink, Jimmy?"

The question stopped him in his tracks.

"And why do you do drugs?"

Jimmy could not move. He could not even face Piper.

"I'll tell you why," said Piper. "You do it because you want to. You do it because you like it. "

Jimmy shook his head.

"Goddamn!" cried Piper. "Just once I'd like to hear somebody admit that they drink because they want to, or do drugs because they want to, or, hell, that they believe in God because they want to. Just once! Come on, Jimmy. Have some pride, man."

Finally, Jimmy turned to face him.

"Pride?"

"Yeah," said Piper. "A little self-esteem. Why don't you tell that other world to go fuck itself once and for all?"

"Is that a joke?" Jimmy cried. "How can I have any pride, man? How can I have any self-esteem? It seems to me that words like those stopped applying to guys like us a long time ago."

Massaging his broken hand, he reflected, "You know, Piper, when I first moved into this house I thought, 'Wow! This is the wildest place on earth. It's so outrageous. So unpredictable.'"

"Yeah?" frowned Piper.

"I used to think that we were so original," Jimmy continued. "I used to think that any two or three days at the HIPPIE HOUSE would make for a great book or movie, but you know what I'm starting to figure out?"

"What?" Piper asked begrudgingly.

"That I've been kidding myself. People have been drinking themselves into oblivion for eons. And it's the same with drugs. Sure, life at the HIPPIE HOUSE is unpredictable, all right. But it's predictably unpredictable, you know? And what's more, if someone actually were to write a book

188

or make a movie about it, it would be the same book or the same movie over and over again. The same exact shit. Now who would want to see that, Piper? Know what I mean?"

"No." Piper was defiant.

"I mean you come here any day and it's really just like any other day. You'll see more people smoking more dope, shooting more coke, popping more pills, drinking more booze, fucking more people. More people more dope more coke more pills more booze more fucking more people. It's a vicious cycle, man. It's a fucking vacuum!"

"Fuck your vacuum!" Piper cut him off. "And fuck you, too!"

"But when is enough enough, Piper?"

"Man!" Piper said lividly. "You're really talking some shit now, Jimmy. You know that? When is enough enough? I'll tell you when. Enough is enough right after you smoke that last bowl. Enough is enough after you drink that last beer. Enough is enough after you snort that last line, after you pop that last pill, after you stick that needle in your arm for the last time and after you fuck that last little seventeen year old debutante who wants to know what life is like on the other side of the tracks! Our side!"

He threw the whiskey bottle at Jimmy. It missed

him, landing harmlessly in the yard instead.

"Hell! Enough – now that's the word that's lost all meaning to guys like you and me."

"And what about The Killer of Love?" said Jimmy. "What does that name mean to guys like you and me?"

Piper smiled. "Why don't you tell me?"

"No," said Jimmy. "I think that that's one riddle everyone has to find the answer to himself, don't you?"

Laughing fiendishly, Piper stood, clapped his hands and pointed at Jimmy.

TWENTY-SIX

"Time to pay the piper," Crazy Don cried menacingly, and Jimmy felt the barrel of the .38 against the back of his skull.

Oddly, he felt more relieved than afraid.

Spinning around, he grinned at Don. "Come on, little man, let's go. Let's do it."

Surprised by his irrational behavior, Don hesitated.

"Come on," Jimmy cried. "What are you waiting on?"

Squinting, Don steadied his aim.

Realizing that the moment was at hand, Jimmy closed his eyes.

The gun discharged.

His eyes jerked wide. Looking down, he saw Piper wrestle Don to the ground and pry the gun from his hands. Grabbing it, he placed the barrel against the bridge of Don's nose and cocked the chamber.

"How does it feel now, Don?" Piper shouted. "Huh?" How does it feel now, you fucking lunatic?"

Don stopped resisting.

"Goddamnit, Don!" continued Piper. "You can't go around shooting people just because your're pissed at 'em. I cleaned up your mess once before and I'm not going to do it again."

"What happened?" Joey demanded as he came running out the front door, Kevin and Harrison close behind.

Looking at Piper, Jimmy could not answer. Instead, he turned and ran down Laurel Avenue.

Wandering aimlessly past the Belle Meade apartments, the Regina condominiums, Laurel High School, the Scottish-Rite Temple, the Carousel, and Vic and Bill's, he felt an overpowering urge to sleep, to just lie down right where he was and go to sleep.

He was so tired! Of thinking, of breathing. Tired of being tired!

"It's getting late," he thought. FANB – 5:01 – 74° – FANB – 5:01 – 74° – FANB – 5:02 – 74°. "It's getting so late!"

Like a nightmare, he found himself at the Grid of Self-knowledge. Soon it would be daylight and something had to be done.

He knew there was only one course of action that would end this misery. Walking onto the beam, he looked down and wondered if the fall would do the job.

Determining that it would, he started to feel a perverse sort of pride for he believed that this act would be the ultimate triumph over Piper. He knew that Piper must have been right where he was now, perhaps once, perhaps a dozen times, and had not had the guts to go through with it. But he, Jimmy Love, would have the courage to end this vampire existence once and for all.

"No," he suddenly rebuked himself. "Accept this for what it is. Don't lie to yourself any longer. Admit just this once that this is no more than the extinguishing of a wisp of stale, putrid air, just like the dust that rises from those big garbage cans down there when Red and Chuck are knocking about in them. Now, shut up and just do it!"

But he hesitated. Wondering what his father would think if he could see him now, he felt ashamed.

Strangely, he recalled the time his father had taken the family out west for their summer vacation when he was still a little boy.

When visiting the Grand Canyon, he saw a bald eagle

for the first time. The most magnificent creature he had ever seen, his father told him that this bird symbolized the freedom of their great nation.

Watching the eagle vault skyward, over the treacherous gorge below, he reverently viewed its impeccable aerial prowess as it glided majestically to and fro.

Yet he was overcome with a sadness.

Yes, even as a child he was gripped by the sadness which sprang from the realization that although he could look upon a spirit as weightless as the eagle whose sings soar upon the winds of change, he would never touch its soul . . . Not even in his dreams.

Confused, he wondered if jumping would be an act of bravery or cowardliness?

"No!" he concluded. "I can't do it! I have to live. I have to fight. It takes courage to fight. It takes courage to live. It will be day soon and this new day will be mine to do with what I will. I will fight, goddamnit! I will live! And what's more, I will change!"

Once again he found himself walking the streets of Fort Sanders. Yet now, he felt a sense of purpose. He thought it fitting that soon the sun would rise and the world would awaken, for he, too, had just awoken from the deepest of sleeps.

FANB – 6:32 – 74°.

Walking on, his eyes fixed on the horizon, he saw an almost imperceptible change. Or was it, perhaps, only his imagination? Stopping, he watched and waited.

His heart soared with wonderment. The day was almost here.

FANB – 6:37 – 74°.

The world was getting brighter by the second. Feeling he had never really lived before this moment, he wondered if this was how other people experienced life.

"Yes!" he decided ecstatically. "We should savor such moments, every moment! We should drink up life like we drink up alcohol. Feel life rushing through our veins like some of us have longed for heroin or cocaine to."

FANB – 6:45 – 75°.

A glimmering from the alley across the street caught his eye.

"What can it be?" he wondered. "A mirror? A pool of water?"

Reaching the source of the reflection, he saw as he stood over it that it was a piece of glass. Bending, he picked it up and examined it.

The glass was very familiar. Its edges told him that someone had discarded it, sending it back to the ground violently to get it to break like this. Still, the part that captured the sunlight was round and perfect. Astonished by its smoothness, he turned it over.

There, still attached to the glass was a label:

Anheiser Busch Brewing Company
St. Louis, Missouri
Budweiser. The King of Beers.
Sixteen Ounces

He swallowed. Then again. His mouth intolerably dry, he was jolted back to reality.

"Oh, God!" he cried. "Why is this happening?"

The sun was much higher in the sky.

FANB – 6:56 – 77°.

Lifting the glass, he saw his reflection. His mouth swollen, his nose inflamed, his eyes were most alarming. Wild and bloodshot, he searched desperately for the soul behind these windows, for the very essence of his existence.

He felt as if an unseen syringe had been jabbed

through his skull and drawn every bit of life-fluid out while he waited, futiley hoping that there was a shot of life-rush out there, somewhere (floating), waiting to be injected into his veins.

He had become the drug: an empty shell, devoid of spirit, devoid of hope, residing in a strange and bitter world where everything was a vast void of darkness, a black hole from which neither light nor matter could escape.

FANB – 7:02 – 77°.

Looking at the glass again, he drew the jagged edge to his wrist and walked deeper and deeper into the Fort.

"Hey wild man," a voice called to him in a muffled tone. "What're you doin' wandering around here this time a the mornin'?"

Weaker now, he saw Red walking towards him from the shadows.

"Say partner," Red grumbled, moving into the street, "you all right? You look a little pale."

The earth spun off its axis. He staggered.

"Say wild man, what's got into you?"

Reaching out, Jimmy bolstered himself against the beggar's shoulder. Reaching into his jeans, he found a dollar bill and offered it to Red.

197

Red stepped back.

"What the . . . ?" he said in astonishment, looking at the blood-soaked money.

Grabbing Jimmy's wrist, he exclaimed, "Jesus! What have you gone and done to yourself, wild man?"

TWENTY-SEVEN

"Eagle One, this is Mission Control. All systems are go. Repeat. All systems are go. Do you copy, Eagle One?"

"Mission Control, this is Eagle One. Affirmative. All systems are go."

"T minus ten, nine, eight, seven. We have ignition. T minus four, three, two, one. We have lift off, Eagle One."

Rocketing skyward, he felt the crushing force of gravity. Watching through a side portal, he saw the blue of the sky whirl by. The earth grew more distant with each passing second. Almost imperceptibly, the horizon grew darker.

"Eagle One, this is Mission Control. We are ready for separation. Do you copy?"

"Affirmative, Mission Control. Eagle One standing by."

The ship separated from its booster with a large thud. He felt isolated and alone.

"Mission Control, this is Eagle One. Do you copy?"

"Affirmative, Eagle One. This is Mission Control. Separation is confirmed. Repeat. Separation is confirmed."

Looking out the window, he felt the vast, cold void of space. Looking down, the blue planet seemed beautiful and mysterious.

He cried out, "Mission Control, this is Eagle One awaiting orders."

There was no answer.

"Mission Control," he said urgently, "this is Eagle One. Do you copy?"

The transmissions began to come in. There was a beeping sound, something akin to Morse code, and then a ringing. Willingly, he received the signals.

He saw himself by the lake making love to Sara, weeping at his father's funeral, fighting in a bar with strangers, smoking a bowl with Piper, slashing at his wrist with a broken beer bottle.

Seeing his wings now, he understood that he was not a real eagle, but a manufactured, man-made eagle. He was a satellite, held to its course by the earth's gravity. All that he was or had ever been was attributable to the signals, which had been transmitted into his brain. And all he ever did or ever could do was simply bounce those transmissions back to the earth.

"Eagle One, this is Mission Control. Do you copy? Eagle One, this is Mission Control. Do you copy? Repeat. Eagle One, this is Mission Control. Do you copy?"

"Don't answer," he told himself. "Just don't answer."

TWENTY-EIGHT

Awaking, the light shining in his eyes was so bright that it made the entire room seem as if he had landed on a beautiful white cloud. Focusing, he saw the sterile, generic white ceiling. Turning his head to one side there was a pole, onto which an intravenous feeding tube was attached. Coughing, he asked himself how this could be.

"Jimmy? Are you awake?" Sara called out to him.

"Thank God," she said as he turned toward her.

He studied her face.

"What is it?" she asked him.

He felt as if he had never seen her in such detail before: her beautiful flowing hair, her long, full lashes and eyebrows, the specks of blue in her green eyes, her nose (smooth and perfect), and her smiling, full lips. Searching his mind for an adjective to describe her beauty, he thought it strange that the only word that entered his mind was 'clean.' Sara seemed clean to him. Immaculate, like this hospital room.

"Jimmy, what is it? Why are you looking at me that way?"

Having grown so accustomed to seeing ugliness, filth, and vileness in his life, he was in a sort of shock at her beauty.

"Clean," he whispered unintelligibly. "Clean."

Pulling up a chair, she explained that a full day and a half had passed since he had been brought to the Emergency Room. She told him that the doctors had not given him much of a chance at first because of the large amount of blood lost, and that they considered him fortunate to be alive.

"Where's Jack and Mom?" he moaned.

"They went downstairs to get a cup of coffee."

An awkward silence ensued. Looking out the window, he saw that it was daylight.

"Jimmy," Sara said at last. "Do you mind if I ask why you did it?"

Turning back to her, he blew out a deep breath.

"It's okay," she said. "You don't have to . . ."

"Do you ever think about her?" he asked. "Do you ever think about our daughter?"

"Of course I do, Jimmy. I think about her all the time."

"I do, too," he said.

"You know," she said, brushing a tear from her eye, "we've all made mistakes, Jimmy. Some more horrible than others. But there comes a time when we just have to let go of the past. Giving up our little girl nearly tore me apart. I thought I'd never get over it. But then I realized that, right or wrong, I had to if I was going to go forward. And the only way to do that was to forgive myself.

"I don't mean that we shouldn't remember. We should because we have to learn from our mistakes and that takes courage. Courage to forgive but not forget. And courage to change, Jimmy. . . . Courage to change."

Struck by the simple truth of her words, he realized how different Sara's wisdom was from Piper's. Her words were so grounded in contrast to his grand philosophies and perverse logic. His rationalizations and distorted reasoning were dark, eternally veiled in the shadow of cynicism, while her simple words of encouragement seemed to shed perfect light on his predicament.

"Jimmy," she continued, "I know that this might not be the time or the place but there's something I've been

204

wanting to say to you for a long time."

He nodded.

"I need you to know that Jack and I never meant to hurt you. You should see him. He's crushed. He thinks he's done this to you."

"Shhh!" Jimmy hushed. "It's okay. Don't cry."

"Oh, Jimmy," she began to sob. "You scared us so badly. Were things really so terrible that you had to try to kill yourself?"

Looking out the window, he started to reply by saying that he had simply run out of hope, but then caught himself.

Thinking of Piper, he groaned shamefully, "I just couldn't live with myself any longer, Sara. I couldn't stand what I had become."

Surprisingly, Sara smiled.

"What?" he asked.

She took his hand.

"Don't you see?" she said. "As long as you're alive, Jimmy, there's still time to change."

Not heeding her call to him that he should not leave the bed, he stood and crossed to the window. Looking outside he saw a large oak tree, and behind it, Fort Sanders. In

205

the distance he saw the clock flash:

FANB – 4:32 – 88°.

Sara's words returned to him.

'As long as you're alive, Jimmy, there's still time to change.'

Thinking of the broken glass with which he had slashed his wrist, he realized that, in one form or another, there would be broken glass in his way every day for the rest of his life.

"That's all right," he thought to himself. "I'm ready to fight!"

Jack and Helen walked in. Thrilled to see Jimmy awake and out of bed, they rushed to his side.

"Jimmy!"

"How are you?"

"How are you feeling?"

Tears began to stream down his cheeks as he hugged them both.

Looking back at Sara, he smiled.

Returning to the window, he thought of Piper and the others down below. His heart felt heavy for them. Watching a car pass on the street and then a flock of black birds scatter from a branch of the oak tree, he saw the clock again.

FANB – 4:33 – 88°.

Noting that it was a minute later than the last time he had looked, he rested his head on the window-pane. Feeling the warmth and light of the sun on his face, he welcomed the passing of time.